MASK OF EMOTIONS

PATH TO DESTINY, BOOK 1

J.L. LAWRENCE

Taylor + April
Everyone must choose their own path.
Choose wisely!

J.L. Lawrence

Cover Design by Rae Monet, Inc.
Edited by Charli Heyer
Interior Layout by Jesse Gordon

DEDICATION

To Kenzie
Your never-ending faith in me is astonishing.
Thank you for listening to all my crazy ideas
and for adding a few of your own.
Love you.

CHAPTER 1

"Cadence Hope Smith."

Seriously? You'd think she'd know my name by now. She'd had this teacher last year. *Twice.*

"Here. And I go by Kate." A group of kids sitting to her left snickered and called her a few insulting and childish names.

I guess tenth grade isn't going to be any better than the last nine years of school.

Ms. Jones nodded, completely ignoring their comments. She might pretend not to notice, but Kate could read her thoughts. She didn't want to start the school year off with a confrontation, so she chose ignorance. Probably didn't help that she'd heard all the stories from Kate's youth and feared her just a little.

Kate rolled her eyes. Maybe she should make more of an effort to get along with the teachers this year and prove she wouldn't divulge their deepest, darkest secrets. She could read every thought in their feeble minds, but, instead, she built impenetrable walls to keep thoughts from getting in or out to protect them.

A lot of good it's done.

It sucked being born with special gifts no one could explain. Her family had gone to great lengths to hide them. In elementary school, all the adults were terrified to get near her. It hadn't helped that she'd outed two affairs, a gambling problem, and a drug addiction before her third-grade year. Wasn't like she meant to, but she'd been too young to control all the thoughts back then. Things had always popped out at the wrong time.

Eventually, she'd gained control and only pried into thoughts when needed. That's why she didn't say anything to the jerks sitting beside her. Only she could know that one of them had a crush on her and his friends were giving him a hard time more than targeting her. Otherwise, she would've given them her famous death stare. While she hadn't had a strange outburst in years, she *did* live in a small town. And no one ever forgot anything—especially the weird stuff.

In other words, *her.*

New names caught her attention. Most of these kids she'd known since birth, and strangers were a rarity.

"Adam Ryan."

"Alyssa Ryan."

Twins with reddish blonde hair, freckled faces, and light blue eyes raised their hands. They sat toward the front. Even though she automatically blocked thoughts now, she still picked up energy from every individual. Not these two. If she wanted to read them, she'd have to make a concentrated effort.

How weird.

Maybe she *should* learn more about them.

The boy, Adam, looked over his shoulder and caught her eye. He winked, then turned back to the teacher. Had he known she'd been thinking about him, or was it a coincidence?

Despite the light hair and eyes, they were both surprisingly tan. Adam wore his hair short and flipped to the side, while his sister had long flowing waves touching the top of her waist. Their features were almost identical with pronounced cheekbones in a round face. The only major difference she'd noticed was their height when they'd collected their textbooks. The brother had a good six inches on his sister.

Luckily, the first day of school required little thinking. All the teachers gave the same spiel of introduction and a get-to-know-you activity. If she heard another teacher utter the word *icebreaker* again, she might scream. Although, it gave her time to study the new kids. Their mental resistance fascinated her, and she stared much more than she should. Sitting toward the back of the room, no one noticed her anyway. That's how she liked it.

Once she'd admitted to herself that only she could make herself fit in with others, she began studying all her classmates' behavior and tried to mimic their multiple attributes. It took a while, but she'd become a master of disguise. Her papa called them her masks.

The bell rang, interrupting her train of thought. Stepping out into the hallway, she took a deep breath. Time to put on the show.

"Kate, come over here." First up, cheerleaders. Their sheer mass of energy overwhelmed her.

"What's up?" She slipped the perfect mask into place.

"There's a party Friday night and we'd love you to join us. You're always so busy. Come have some fun with us." Sally, head cheerleader and fashionista, bounced around her.

Kate harnessed her mental energy. Whenever she joined them, she used compulsion to help them see the perfect version of herself. Her dirty-blonde hair always appeared perfect, flowing down past her shoulders. Manicured nails and flawless makeup rounded out the deception. She'd even adapted her clothing to fit the latest trends and learned how to subdue her unusually bright blue eyes.

Amazing how easy it'd become to trick the human mind.

"I'd love to. Text me the details and location. I'll do my best to stop by."

"Great!" Sally jumped up and down, then hugged her.

They continued to walk and laugh together until she went into her next class.

Breathing a sigh of relief, she released the facade for a minute. She headed to the back of the classroom where she could fade into the scenery. The new twins caught her attention. Two classes in a row. This time they sat in the back near her. Totally weird. Since there was only one county high school, it maintained quite a high number of students. Repeat classes were a rarity especially considering she was a sophomore taking mostly junior classes.

Every time she looked up, one of them had been watching. If they wanted to be friends, they were off to a creepy start. Kate focused her eyes on Mr. Majors. Sweet man, but the most boring history teacher on the planet. At least most of his assignments were straight forward and he didn't require any group projects. A big plus in her opinion.

The next dismissal bell cued her next mask. She'd convinced her school counselor that an independent study hall would be perfect to maintain her grades in all her advanced academic courses. It'd taken a little persuasion on her part since juniors and seniors were the only ones allowed study halls. She dropped by guidance and waved to be marked for attendance. They didn't track her beyond that.

On her way to the lunchroom, someone grabbed her shoulder from behind. Wesley, the star quarterback winked at her. She smiled, becoming the friend he expected. "You're in a good mood today, Wes."

"Look, I know it's the first day and all, but I already know my chemistry teacher is a killer. I can't let my grades drop this year. Any way you'd be willing to help one afternoon a week like last year?"

She hid her sigh. Being academically ahead of most students her age wasn't always a positive. Everyone needed something from her. Maybe she should learn to say *no* more, but Wes and his friends had helped her begin to fit in. Their behavior had been the easiest to duplicate. Once she'd established the *no touching or looking* policy and reinforced it in their minds, they'd become pretty good acquaintances. It also got her mom off her back.

"Sure, Wes. How about Thursdays again?"

He nodded and gave her a quick hug. She tried not to cringe, but she hated being touched. Their emotions spilled over and into her. Hopes, dreams, doubts, and fears all stormed her mind. She threw up mental blocks to prevent the majority and carefully controlled her emotions. Smiling, she patted his shoulder in return and stepped back.

"You're the best, Kate. See you Thursday." He disappeared into the hordes of students running to their next class.

Turning the corner, she ran straight into the band kids. Her morning emotional turnaround gave her whiplash. Although, if she had to pick a school group she liked best, it'd be them. They were strange at times and oddly obsessive about music, but also genuine. They accepted everyone into their clique, quirks and all. Too bad she couldn't play an instrument to save her life. And singing wasn't an option. One accidental compulsion and she'd drive the audience to do something crazy. She'd been told once that she possessed a killer voice. They didn't know how accurate that could be.

"Hey, what's up, Kate? How'd your summer go?" Kenzie ran up to her but, thankfully, didn't hug her. She played the baritone and adored marching band. Kate didn't care for carrying around a heavy instrument for several hours, but admired Kenzie's dedication.

"Pretty boring. Spent time with a few friends, did some babysitting, and hung around home." Well, the staying home and working part had some truth in it. Mostly, she'd read books and dreamed of all the places she would go when she escaped this stupid town. And she'd continued to master her abilities. One day she'd make them completely disappear.

"Sounds cool. I didn't do much either, other than the band trip to Washington D.C. for the Fourth of July Parade. Way hot, but fun."

"Awesome! Tell me more."

Kenzie walked with her the rest of the way to the lunchroom telling her all about the adventure. She envied that kind of freedom and fun. Kenzie joined her friends in the lunchroom, but they talked to her for a moment and asked about her summer and classes before she finally broke free.

Lunch had become her de-stress time. In order to be the person everyone wanted her to be, she exerted a ton of energy. In the lunchroom, she sent out mental *do not disturb* waves and always chose a small table in the back. At least her school offered great salads every day. So, she picked up her meal and headed to her isolated spot. Her mind drifted to all the adventures she'd have someday.

"May we join you?"

What the...? No one ever interrupted her or got past her compulsion.

The twins stared back at her. Great, now even her lunch didn't provide a sanctuary. Were they sent here to torture her?

She projected calm, cool, collected Kate. "I usually eat alone. It gives me time to think and read. I guess you can join me today, since you're new and all." She'd stay long enough not to be rude, then excuse herself to the library. Her other sanctuary. Hopefully, they wouldn't invade it, too. She motioned them to sit.

"I'm Alyssa and this is my brother, Adam. It's Kate, right?"

"Yeah, that's me."

"You know, you wouldn't need as much rest if you didn't use so much energy trying to fit in with everyone. Your aura is all over the place. You even changed your outward appearance —or at least what they interpreted as your appearance—several times. Must be exhausting. Just so you know, you can be yourself with us. My brother and I tend to see past the dog and pony show."

Kate couldn't form words. Who the heck were these people and how dare this new girl think she knew anything about her or her struggles? Her brother stared intently and didn't seem fazed by his sister's words. One thing was certain. If they knew the depth of her weirdness, no way would they want her to be herself.

Racking her brain, she tried to think of a polite response and hasty exit. "Thank you, but my aura is just fine, as is the rest of me."

"Suit yourself. But you'd be a lot happier if you stopped pretending to be someone else. I'm not trying to be rude, but we've been where you are and learned the hard way. Acceptance will bring about the full use of your abilities. Can you move stuff with your mind?" Her brother sent her a stern look, and from the flinch on her face, must have kicked her under the table.

Where did these people come from? Straight off the crazy train would be her guess. Like she would discuss anything in this gossip-hungry school. She had to get out of here before everything she'd built over the last few years came tumbling down.

"I'm not sure what you're talking about. But even if I did, this isn't the time or place to ever discuss it. The walls have ears. I appreciate your concern, but my aura, friends, and all other aspects of my life are just as I want them. It was nice meeting you both. I have to head to my independent study assignment. Good luck this school year." Kate hoped it sounded like a polite but solid dismissal.

A rebellious piece of her couldn't resist responding to their insinuations. She focused on Alyssa's drink and made it move to the left as she reached for it. Kate anticipated seeing shock or fear at what she'd done, but Alyssa smirked and nodded like she'd expected it to happen.

Turning on her heels, Kate sprinted to the library.

The library wing had been donated by a rich old lady about fifteen years ago. She'd had a strong love for books and no family. So, they'd built a two-story addition to the high school in her name. It probably had more books than the public library and definitely had fewer kids running around.

"Hello, Kate. I'm headed to lunch. The place is yours."

"Thanks, Ms. Coby. I'll keep an eye on things."

She smiled. "I'm sure you will while you're immersed in those books of yours. By the way, I received some new fantasy novels yesterday. Take a look. Let me know what you think."

Ms. Coby had known her family for years. She'd even briefly been at her elementary school. Funny how she'd never felt any fear toward Kate, and luckily allowed her to have the library to herself. Ms. Coby only allowed her to visit during lunch because she didn't want students hiding upstairs and making out. She had a valid point.

Climbing the stairs, she let the silence and peace surround her. The twins could become a complication, but she'd handle it. She'd had years to perfect the persona the world saw, and no one could change that.

She picked up one of the new books, trying to put all the other stuff out of mind, but her thoughts kept going back to the strange conversation in the cafeteria. What had Alyssa meant by her aura? She didn't have a clue what that meant. Could others see it? Was she at risk?

Finally, she gave up on reading and went to find her secret stash of books. An elderly lady with no family had passed years ago and had donated her books in addition to her money. Some dealing with witchcraft, healing arts, or other uncomfortable subject matter that had been deemed inappropriate remained hidden away in storage.

When she'd helped clean up the storage rooms last year, she'd accidentally found them. Why Ms. Coby hadn't thrown them away she'd never know, but Kate had hidden them away to see if she could find an answer for her abilities. Or at least how to get rid of them. No luck with either so far. But she did remember seeing a book on auras. Seemed like a good time to get better acquainted. Next time, she wouldn't be caught off guard.

The dark brown armchair welcomed her, so she sank into it. Opening the book, she began to read about all the different colors that could surround a person within their energy field. She'd noticed it, but didn't understand it. After a little more reading she decided this seemed like a good tool to have.

She'd always labeled her gifts into two columns: Can live with it, and Want to get rid of it. Truthfully, most of her abilities bounced back and forth, depending on the day and situation. Reading thoughts definitely caused a problem, but she loved her mental compartments. She could store away memories, thoughts, emotions, or anything else, like a filing cabinet inside her head. If she ever wanted access, she could relive them as if they'd just happened.

Anything she didn't want to think about or feel, she could lock away. It had become her favorite ability and the one she wouldn't willingly give up. Her ability to camouflage and fade into her surroundings was useful, but she could live without it. Compulsion was the most dangerous of them all.

Her words could influence other's actions. If she concentrated, people around her would do whatever she suggested.

She could sing it or speak it, which was why she couldn't join the chorus. What if she sang a love song and accidentally caused the entire student body and faculty to become lovesick idiots? Not a risk she could take.

When she was young, her papa had told her many times that, with great power came great responsibility. She'd gladly give hers to someone else, but it seemed to be her eternal burden.

Snapping the book closed, she took a deep breath. The book had provided several methods to improve her techniques, but none to remove it. However, the skill did have a lot of potential. She needed to read more on the subject, so she'd have to find a way to get more books. At least she'd gained enough sense over the years to know she couldn't play around with her abilities. She'd caused enough heartbreak as a child. Even her own mother feared her, and her dad rarely spoke to her. If not for her papa, no telling where she'd be in this world.

Goosebumps broke out across her arm and her neck tingled. She glanced up, but saw no one. "Is someone there?"

No response. She stood and took a quick look around, then opened her mind to see who had intruded. She came up empty. After checking one more time, she returned the books to her hiding spot.

She tried to shake off the uneasy feeling in her gut, but she'd bet her life, someone was watching her. She didn't feel danger, but who knew what kind of crazies lurked in this school? She looked around several more times. No one appeared.

Maybe, I'm going crazy.

"I need to chill out," she muttered and gathered her belongings. Time to head to her last class for the day.

Letting go of her suspicions, she returned her thoughts to the first day a school. Success or failure? Overall, not bad. Her masks were still successful and no one suspected her of anything crazy. Except the twins.

Adam and Alyssa.

Maybe she'd scared them off and they'd leave her alone. She rushed to class to avoid the tardy bell.

Guess I'll find out tomorrow.

She didn't have to wait that long. The minute she sat down, they sat on either side of her. If she didn't know better, she'd have sworn they were intentionally pestering her. She locked down her mind and emotions. She needed distance and had never looked forward to going home this much in her entire life.

This could be a very long year.

CHAPTER 2

Kate punched the bag with every ounce of her strength. Adam and Alyssa not only had every class with her, including a study hall, but had insisted on sitting with her at lunch all week. Why couldn't they take the hint? Most days she'd ended up going to the library to hide. But she still couldn't shake the feeling of being watched.

The thud of her hand against the plastic punching bag echoed in the studio. She'd earned her black belt years ago in middle school at a time when she'd had anger control issues. Her papa had insisted on a proper outlet and her mother had finally agreed. This is where she'd learned to control all the crazy emotions, especially anger. The compartments had saved her and allowed her to maintain complete control. She still slipped every once in a while, but she'd found freedom and let go of fear and resentment.

Sparring allowed her to release all the stress and pent-up frustration. While she'd decided not to join the competitive circuit, she didn't hold back during practice. Only the instructors seriously sparred with her now. The other students no longer provided a challenge, so she became their mentor.

The master instructor had asked her to join him and some of the other students every summer for a world karate tour to increase her knowledge, but she'd always declined. Being confined with a group of people taxed her energy levels. Maybe one day she could control it and go. It'd still be nice to have a real challenge and, at least, one person on her level.

Since she hadn't put on all her gear yet, an open spot on the mats beckoned her. She closed her mind and focused on the patterns etched in her heart. The first pattern she'd ever learned flowed through her. She continued each additional set until the world around her disappeared. Precise movements combined with purpose brought structure to her insane life. For a brief moment, she controlled every action. Strength rippled through her, and peace calmed her soul.

The doorbell caught her attention, and goosebumps broke out across her arms. She cast a look over her shoulder. Someone up above had a funky sense of humor.

Adam strode inside and stared right at her. The black belt circling his waist let her know he wasn't a newbie. Still, she briefly wondered where to draw the line with stalkers. No way this was all a coincidence. Not possible, but then what else could it mean? She didn't want to know. In her lifetime, she'd learned answers were sometimes worse than unanswered questions.

He approached her and nodded toward the mats. "How 'bout it?"

What'd she have to lose? "Fine, but no talking. Stay focused."

Laughing, he headed to the floor. "You're the boss."

Her instructor nodded his approval and pointed toward the side room. He intended to give them space, but everyone had too much curiosity for their own good. She'd remember that the next time they asked her to go easy on them.

His eyes never left hers. The intensity unnerved her. Maybe that was his game plan. Didn't matter. She had no intention of going down in front of her peers.

He lifted his fist pads, and they bumped them in respect, then turned to the lead instructor monitoring the match. They bowed, faced each other, and bowed again.

Time to go. She squared her shoulders. Not wanting to give him an advantage, she launched immediately. Double punch followed by a side kick. He evaded them easily.

He returned with his own advance. She blocked his kick and ducked his punch. His movements were precise and quick. Staying on her toes, she moved around the floor to maintain her position. Their skill level proved to be equal and their attack resembled a choreographed dance. She admired his abilities. Pale blue eyes met hers in total determination to win.

"You look a little nervous, Kate," Adam smirked, obviously trying to distract her. "Never lost before?"

"Not in a long time, and I'm not planning to break tradition today."

Doubling her efforts, she let the inner controls fade and forced the clutter from her mind. Her focus became razor sharp as she embraced her surroundings and remembered all she'd been taught. This was her house. Electricity shimmered through her blood as the adrenaline pumped.

He tried to sweep her legs but she jumped over him. He rolled and popped back up. She aimed a flying kick at his head, but he grabbed her leg and flung her down. Before he could regain his balance for his next move, she swept his legs and he hit the floor. He landed beside her.

Pain radiated across her lower back. It was a humbling experience and not one she cared to repeat. She jumped to her feet as did he. He didn't appear very winded, and she tried to hide her own deep breaths.

Enough.

Drawing in every ounce of strength and energy, she advanced. She danced across the floor throwing at least a dozen roundhouse kicks, forcing him to retreat and block. When they approached the edge of the mat, she switched legs and sent a high kick toward his head. He blocked but wasn't prepared for her to flip backward, extending her leg in the air, connecting with his chin.

He stumbled back. She pressed her advantage, dropping an elbow to his midsection and sweeping his legs. He tried to jump up, but she knocked him down. She swung her hand in a downward motion across his neck, claiming the victory.

The instructor announced her as the winner and everyone in the studio cheered. Then he returned them all to class. Both Kate and Adam remained on the ground for several minutes, catching their breath. At least, he'd given her a challenge. Next time, he might even beat her. She'd taken him by surprise with her abilities today, but he probably wouldn't be unprepared again. He could push her to become better. Exactly what she'd wished for. She'd be more careful with those wishes in the future.

They stayed silent while taking off all their padding. Before he could start a conversation, she darted from the floor into the locker room. A little cowardly on her part, but she didn't feel up for any more of his probing questions. She'd had enough of that at school this week.

She waited several minutes, hoping he'd left. Peeking her head around the corner, the coast appeared clear. With a deep breath, she walked to the front of the studio, sat down on one of the black leather couches, and sank into the worn leather. They were mostly to offer parents comfort while waiting to pick up their kids, but she used them for quiet reading time.

Adam plopped down beside her, squishing her to the side. "What'cha reading?"

She counted to ten. Then counted again. But he hadn't taken the hint. "A new mystery series. I thought you'd left."

"Nah. I had to finish up some paperwork in the office. I like it here. The master instructor seems knowledgeable and highly skilled."

"Yeah, he's also the owner and has connections all over the world. We're pretty lucky to have that kind of caliber in such a small town." Safe conversation, and she did love this place. It'd become another home for her.

Kate nodded toward the exit. "Are you waiting on your parents to pick you up?"

He shook his head. "No, Alyssa is supposed to be here. I'm sure she got caught up shopping somewhere."

"How old is she?"

"*We're* sixteen. We have an August birthday, so our parents decided to have us wait an extra year before starting school. It has advantages, like having a license before our other classmates. What about you?"

"I'm only fifteen, so I have a learner's permit. I can't wait to have my license, but it'll have to wait a while. June birthday for me."

He walked to the windows, looking for his sister. "Do your parents pick you up?"

"No, I catch a ride with one of the instructors. He's on floor two." She pointed upward. It gave her mom one less thing to complain about.

Adam's face went blank. She swore she saw irritation in his stare. "Is he your boyfriend?"

She snorted. "Absolutely not. I don't date much." *Not at all.* "He lives close to my house and helps me out. Not that it's any of your business."

He craned his neck toward the window. "Alyssa's pulling in. Why don't *we* give you a ride home? We can grab some dinner, and you won't have to wait an hour or more."

Come into my parlor said the spider to the fly. Or had paranoia overtaken her mind? She'd been reading the twins all week and hadn't noticed any danger. They seemed to genuinely want to be friends. Secretly, she wanted that, too. *Real* friendship. Maybe if she spent some more time with them, she could see if it would be possible.

Deciding to throw caution to the wind and see what made the twins tick, she nodded. "Ok, I'll let Brian know and meet you outside."

"I'll carry your backpack out to the car." Adam slung it over his shoulder.

She shrugged and went toward the back room. Guess he didn't trust her not to bolt again. But her curiosity had been piqued. She only hoped it didn't get her hurt. Or worse.

Alyssa squeaked as she approached the car. "I'm so glad Adam convinced you to let us take you home. I know he mentioned stopping for dinner, but Mom just called and said it's spaghetti night. A specialty of hers. Want to join us? She said it'd be alright."

So, she'd gone from a ride home and quick bite to eat, to having dinner in their home. Not quite the public safe place she'd envisioned to learn more about them. On the other hand, they might be more relaxed, and she'd gain a lot of useful information.

Pushing doubts aside, she accepted. She called her mom and told her she'd be hanging out with friends. She gave her the address, just in case. Her mother actually sounded relieved. In the back of her mind, she couldn't shake the nervousness or the old saying that curiosity killed the cat. One of her mother's favorite warnings. And her favorite response to her mother was that satisfaction brought it back. Then again, cats had nine lives and she only had one.

She buckled her seat belt and said a silent prayer. What had she gotten herself into?

Alyssa pulled into a long driveway. Kate figured they only lived about five minutes from her own house and formulated how long it would take to run home. Best to be prepared.

The trees cleared and a beautiful ranch style house captured her attention.

An amazing porch stretched across their home with white columns going down into a brick base. The house itself was rustic red with gray shutters surrounding the windows. The porch lights gave off a soft glow, beckoning her inside. She scanned everything around her but didn't feel any danger. Her gifts better not fail her now. If she had to live with them, they should, at least, protect her. Hopefully.

She followed Adam and Alyssa up the steps to the front door. It appeared normal. She glanced twice at the welcome mat. Had the words changed? *No.* Her imagination was out of control. Taking several deep breaths, she reined in the nerves and paid attention to the details of the house.

They walked into a mudroom and took off their shoes. Adam dropped his backpack on the bench to the right. The area opened into the living room. She didn't like meeting new people, so she steeled herself for the inevitable backlash of curiosity and emotions.

A man, she assumed to be their dad, walked in and shook her hand. Surprisingly, his thoughts didn't overwhelm. She merely felt genuine interest. Who were these people? How did they all have such amazing control over their minds? Could they teach her mother?

"It's nice to meet you, Kate. I'm Luke. The kids have been talking about you all week. Glad to put a face to the name. Come on into the dining room. Linda's almost done, so we can grab a seat." He motioned for her to follow.

So far, so good. No alarming weirdness except their unusual calm around her. Maybe they hadn't heard all the rumors and old stories. Parents usually didn't like her hanging around their house. Too many secrets.

This family seemed open and honest. She'd enjoy it while it lasted. Adam bumped her shoulder. "Stop being so suspicious and relax. You're safe here. Everyone is accepted for all their talents, including you." He guided her into the seat beside his. Alyssa sat across from her.

Another set of boy/girl twins stormed the room. They were a few years younger but almost identical to their older siblings. Adam motioned for them to calm down. "These little goons are Ally and Andy. My mom has a thing for 'A' names."

Apparently. "It's nice to meet you." While their thoughts and emotions were less contained, they were still protected. Crazy to have that much skill at a young age. Most *adults* she knew struggled with control.

Their mom and dad walked in carrying plates. The pasta sauce and light garlic scent filled the air. Her mouth watered, but she waited until everyone had been served. They definitely had manners covered. Once all the food had been provided, Linda, who'd introduced herself while delivering the plates, nodded for everyone to join hands.

Adam's hand created a tingle in her own. She couldn't pull away, but shut down the feelings really quick and focused on the little girl squirming on her other side. Luke said grace and they began to eat. Everyone must have been starved because no one spoke for a full ten minutes. It gave her a little time to process her surroundings and take in more of the family dynamics and the home.

The dining room set had to be antique. Her papa loved to restore old furniture and had built several of his own pieces. She recognized the craftsmanship and finishing she'd seen from other expensive sets. The china cabinet had astonishing detail and had been kept immaculate. Probably a family heirloom. The only thing her biological dad had left her was a weird necklace that she'd only seen once. Then her mother had freaked out, so she'd never asked again. Didn't matter. She'd never meet the man.

Once appetites became satisfied, the conversation began. Mostly, the parents asked about their day. Alyssa brought up that Kate had bested Adam in sparring. His dad looked particularly amused. She enjoyed the banter and the obvious love between all the family members. She envied their relationship.

"So, Kate, what other abilities do you have other than reading minds? Who provides your training?" Linda nonchalantly threw in the question while passing more food to her youngest.

Do what? She stayed silent not knowing how to respond. She'd never been asked point blank what she could do.

Alyssa jumped to her defense. "Mom, her family isn't like ours. They keep everything hidden. And I suspect training hasn't been an option. Right?"

Honesty or lying? Which would be better? "I always try to be normal. I bury everything else as deep as I can, so I can survive in the world around me." A strong neutral option.

Linda leaned forward. "What defines *normal*, dear? You've been given wonderful gifts. With these abilities, I would guess a great destiny awaits you. It's best to know what you have and how to control it. Then, how much you use it is up to you. Have you ever caused an accident or embarrassment?"

"Many times, but I've learned to suppress it, so I don't hurt anyone ever again."

"But with control, that would no longer be a fear. We are a family of many talents. My intention isn't to overwhelm you today, but I'd like to help you if you'll let me. No pressure. Just know if you have questions, you're not alone." Kate had to admit that sounded pretty great. She wasn't ready to divulge all her secrets quite yet, though.

The entire family nodded in support. What a different life they'd led. "Thank you. As I'm sure Adam and Alyssa have told you, I can read thoughts and emotions. When I focus, I can see colors around the individual, which I've recently become aware of as auras. I sense danger and truth. It took me a long time to lock all this away."

Linda walked up behind her and laid a hand on her shoulder. "With training and experience, you won't have to hide it. You can control it. Something to think about."

Maybe she had a point. If she really wanted complete control, she needed to understand. She didn't have the guts to tell them about her ability of compulsion, levitation, or blending. She didn't mind sharing a few gifts, but not that she was a full-out freak of nature. They hadn't developed enough trust between them yet, and she feared their judgment.

Should she give this friendship a chance, or run away? She didn't have a clue and didn't have anyone to talk to. And she desperately wanted someone she could trust to talk to about all this stuff happening to her.

"Since you took a chance and were honest with us, it's only fair we return the favor." Linda had taken her seat again, but held her gaze. "My family has similar gifts. We are all telepathic, telekinetic, study auras, and practice many of the Wiccan beliefs."

Say what? Witchcraft? What had she gotten herself into? She couldn't respond because she didn't know where to begin.

Adam gritted his teeth. "Mom, you're scaring her. What my mom means is that we've learned to be open about many things that occur in this universe. We don't do crazy rituals or sacrifices. We're honestly not scary, so just give us a chance. You'll always be safe with us. With *me*." He took her hand and met her eyes. "Always."

Alyssa reached across the table joining her hand to theirs. "Ditto. We've got your back, Kate. We only want to be great friends who rely on each other when the world gets tough. If you'll let us." Her sincerity spoke to Kate deep inside and answered her prayers for someone to understand the weight she carried.

Adam laced his fingers through hers, and it caused her stomach to flip. She didn't have time for romance, so she tried to pull away, but he held on tightly. She needed to think and sort through all the information overload. Were they for real? Could she trust them? If they turned out to be fake in any way, it would crush her heart. Not many in this world had earned that level of trust from her. Actually, only one.

Papa.

This could open a whole new world or bring about her destruction. Time to make one of her infamous pro-con lists.

Kate smiled and reassured Adam and Alyssa, who seemed genuinely upset by her silence. "Dinner was amazing. Thank you for inviting me. I appreciate the honesty and love I see in your family. I haven't been raised with the same advantages, so I need a little time to process. And my mother will be getting worried soon, so I need to get home. But I want you to know I enjoyed myself tonight, for the first time in a long time."

"I'll drive you." Adam jumped up from the table. "I didn't realize the time. Be back in a few minutes, Mom." He grabbed the keys from the entryway table but didn't let go of her hand. Maybe he thought she'd run if he let go.

"No rush. Alyssa can help with the dishes."

Alyssa started to say something but her mom pulled her into the kitchen. She yelled a quick goodbye before she went through the doorway.

Kate's nerves had gotten the best of her. Butterflies churned in her stomach as Adam drove closer to her home. They sat in silence for most of the drive, then about a mile away from her house, he pulled over on the shoulder. She couldn't prevent the immediate alarm and clammy hands while she sorted through the situation.

He unlatched his seatbelt and shifted to face her. "Look, Kate. I know we bombarded you tonight about things you've been burying for a long time. You don't have to accept everything today, just give us a chance. We've been through feeling like outcasts and trying to accept who we are. I've been lucky to have a supportive family and a sister who's beside me every step of the way. My mom recognized that piece is missing for you and overstepped a tad. I'm sorry about that. Don't shut us out. Please?" He reached for her hand and laced their fingers again.

He appeared as nervous as she felt. He cleared his throat. "I like you." It seemed he struggled with every word. "I have since we first met, but I heard you when you mentioned that you don't date. I'd like to change your mind. I also understand why you made that decision. I've failed miserably at dating in the past. So, what I'd like is for the three of us to hang out and spend time together. Build trust. I'll never pressure you, but I'd like the chance to know you better."

His words were wise beyond his years like he'd lived a million lifetimes. Her mind whirled with all the possibilities, but he had a point. They could try to build trust and see where the road led. She'd never been a coward and didn't want to start now.

Leaning against his shoulder, she stared down at their intertwined fingers. "I think starting as friends is a good idea. I'd be lying if I said I'm not attracted to you. And you probably know it, so honesty is my best option. I've built up a ton of walls for good reasons. I can't afford to get distracted and lose everything I've worked for or embarrass my family again. As for us hanging out, I'd like that. Can you give me a little time to sort through it all?" She hesitantly asked the question, finally meeting his eyes.

He stroked her cheek with his free hand. "Of course. I'm all about giving you time or whatever you need. Just don't shut me out. Promise?"

"Promise." The silence stretched as they gazed into each other's eyes. Both fighting the desire to lean in for a first kiss. He finally moved away and pulled the car back onto the road. He turned into her driveway a couple of minutes later.

"See you Monday, Blondie."

She shook her head and gave him a warning look. "Monday. I'll be there." She hesitated. Part of her wanted to seal her heart and block all emotion. The other part wanted to embrace the new feelings and explore. She had a lot of sorting to do. With a sigh, she stepped out and shut the door. Excitement ran through her, and a new awareness began to take hold.

"Who are these people?" Her mother's voice grew louder with each syllable. "I've never heard of that family. How do we know they're not some crazies trying to take advantage of a young girl? And you let that boy drive you home alone? How old is he?"

Kate should've known a fight was inevitable. "Mother, I'm fully capable of protecting myself. And you know better than most that I can take care of myself physically and mentally. Besides, I know they won't hurt me." Kate crossed her arms and straightened her back in preparation for the usual explosion.

Her mother's eyes went wild. "You don't know anything. I've warned you several times to never mention any of that mental crap. You are *normal*. That's all there is to it. Do you hear me? *Normal!*"

Kate had finally had enough. "The whole neighborhood heard your crazy screaming! They're beginning to think you're as messed up as me. Maybe more. Isn't that a riot?"

Lowering her head, she tried to regain her calm. Her mother simply couldn't understand and never would. "Mom…" She made a conscious effort to soften her voice. "Our fights are becoming worse because you refuse to accept what I am. One day, I'm going to walk out that door, and I won't return. You haven't made this a home I'd want to come back to. I have three years left of high school and my bags are packed. All I ask for is peace until then. Yet, I know that's the one thing you can't give me. Why do you always try to deny everything I am? Can't you tell how hard it is for me to be who you want me to be?"

Tears filled her mother's eyes. "I just want you to be safe and have a normal life. I love you, Kate. If you don't get rid of them, these things that make you different will eventually ruin your life. It's why I push so hard. I go to bed every night fearing what the next day will bring for you. You're my only child. Why is so wrong for me to want a good future for you? A career, a family, a home."

"You're shoving me right out the door. I love you, too, but we'll never agree on this. Our minds are wired differently. You want to me to hide from the world, and I want to save it. Or at least save one person at a time. I've felt this calling all of my life. I swear I was born with the need to help others. At some point, you'll have to accept me or let me go." She went to her room and shut the door.

She couldn't stay in this house tonight. Picking up her phone, she dialed the one person who loved her no matter what. She needed that tonight. "Papa, it's been one of those days. Can you come get me?"

"Another fight with your mother?"

"Yes, I need space and to talk to you about some other things." The knot in her chest had already begun to loosen.

"I'll be there in fifteen minutes. Why don't you plan to stay the weekend? Give everyone a chance to cool down." His gruff voice brought her comfort.

"I'm already packed. See you soon. Love you." She moved quickly and waited outside.

Each minute took an eternity. Living on a farm had its advantages. She passed the time counting the cattle and horses as they lazily walked around the fields. They had it easy. Unlike her, they weren't burdened with expectations.

CHAPTER 3

Fog swirled at Kate's feet, and the mist folded around her like a warm coat. The familiar dark forest loomed ahead. Every night she returned to this ominous place. To this man. He stood hidden in the shadows, and she felt him searching for her. He called out, but she couldn't understand his words. His anger had built over the years.

He weaved in and out of trees in the distance, moving closer, searching for her. Why couldn't he see her? Holding out his hand, he beckoned her to join him. A tattoo on his arm glowed in the night. The only part of the man she could ever see clearly. Whenever it lit up, the urge to follow him into the woods pulled deep inside her. Sometimes she sensed a profound desperation within him. Why did he need her? Maybe he needed help.

She wanted to see his face, but only the tattoo shined in the dark. A shield stretched across his forearm with wings sticking out of either side. Could be angel's wings or a rare bird of some sort. Specks of gold created a mystical illusion within them. A sword sliced through the middle. Small symbols were etched on the shield but weren't clear enough for her to completely make out.

Should she follow the strange man into the mist this time? Would he protect her or kill her? Was he good or evil? She didn't know, but a large piece of her wanted to find out. She took a hesitant step forward and froze. Maybe she'd find her destiny, or maybe she'd find death.

Taking a step back, she, once again, turned away from the man in the mist. Just as she had every night of her life. One day she'd find the courage, but not today.

Tears flowed down her cheeks. A strange sadness settled within her. When would this go away? What did these visions want from her?

The lights in the sky captured her attention. She knew the drill. This signaled the end of the journey. Now, she stood in front of an ocean. Wings like a mythical phoenix spanned the width of her vision. Two swords crossed in the middle surrounded by blue and reddish orange flames. Some type of plant-like ivy crept up the blades. In the center, several symbols she didn't understand competed the scene.

It rushed toward her and shot through her body. A voice whispered in her ear telling her to be patient. *Her destiny awaits*. What did that mean? Why couldn't she get rid of these dreams that had haunted her every night of her life? She struggled to breathe and fought the fog encasing her.

Kate gasped for air, then sighed in relief. Her familiar bed and furniture surrounded her. One of these days, she feared she'd wake up on the other side of the rainbow or in a looney bin. She needed a therapist who would listen and not lock her up.

The clock beside her flashed seven in the morning. Too early for a Saturday. Just once, she'd love to sleep late. But the dream never rested, so neither did she.

The smell of coffee signaled Papa had already started his day. Groaning, she rolled out of bed and trudged into the kitchen. She probably looked like a total wreck with her hair sticking out in all directions, but she didn't care. Who'd she have to impress? Papa had never been one to mention her appearance and her grandmother had already left to visit some friends.

She plopped down into the chair beside him and let out a long sigh, baiting him to open the conversation that she hated to start.

"Rough night, Katie girl?"

"You could say that."

"Did you have the dream again?"

"That obvious, huh? Yeah, it won't go away no matter what I try. Even when I'm sick and take medicine that makes me sleepy, the dream cuts through. I'm not sure what to do any-more. What does it want from me?" She laid her head down on the table.

Papa patted her shoulder. "I don't know the answer to that, but you're strong enough to face it. Having to 'face it' being the operative part of that."

"I don't want to deal with it or have anything to do with it. My wish is to be normal. Maybe then I wouldn't be hated by everyone around me."

"Kate, stop the pity party. People don't hate you. You've cre-ated a nice life for yourself. Sometimes you forget we live in a small town. I hear all the other grandparents talk about what an amazing friend you are and how you help everyone. Not that I agree with the multiple personas you show the world, but you've managed to fit in fine, despite the unusual nature of your life. The real issues are finding someone to see past the il-lusion and trusting yourself to let go of the masks. I know the dream didn't affect you that much. So, spill it. Is this about the fight with your mother?"

He never let her take the easy way out. Probably what had kept her sane. "Partly. It's still obvious she doesn't accept who or what I am. I'm already planning my escape after graduation.

I'll miss you, of course, but I've got to find a place that isn't tainted with my past."

He stayed quiet for a moment, then reached over and tipped up her chin to meet her eyes. "Your past is not tainted, Kate. It's all in your mind. Unfortunately, your mother created a lot of those doubts because of her own fears. You struggle so hard to fit in that you don't realize all teenagers go through this phase."

"Yeah, but most can't force others to speak the truth or read all their secrets."

"Yet, you've learned to control it. Others have their own inner demons. It doesn't make it any less traumatic for them. Everything happens for a reason. You know this even if you hide from it at times. So, what else is upsetting you? You and your mother fight like cats and dogs at least once a week. Not a lot new there."

Should she tell him about the new kids? Why not? They didn't keep secrets from each other. "I wouldn't say upsetting as much as intriguing. There are these new students at school. They spotted my abilities right away and appear to have some of their own. I'm not sure whether or not it's safe to be friends with them. As you said, I've created a world I can function within. If it's destroyed, I'm not sure I can go through another building process." She told him about their questions, the sparring match, and dinner at their house.

When she started to describe their mother's openness and willingness to help, he raised an eyebrow, but let her finish. No condemnation. Her mother would be calling the neighborhood watch and gathering a mob by now to chase them out of town. Her Papa's reactions surprised her at times, like he knew so much more about this world than he'd say.

"Kate, I think you *should* trust them and befriend them. Sometimes, fate or our guardian angels send us what we need most to cope with life. As you grow older and become your own person, the fights with your mother won't go away. She knows time's running out, and she's holding on too tightly. You've never had friends who know the whole you. I'm the only one you talk to about any of this, and I can't live forever."

"Papa, please don't say things like that. You know it causes me even more anxiety."

He sighed and patted her shoulder. "I'm only saying what's true. Building friendships will provide a genuine circle of safety and acceptance, as well as happiness. Are these two the ultimate friends of a lifetime? I don't know. Maybe they're simply guides along life's journey. But I think all of you deserve a chance to find out. And their mother's acceptance is hard for you to understand, but what if your children bear the same abilities? Imagine what you could learn from her example?"

No wonder she liked being with him. He always made sense of things. "I hope having kids is *way* down the line."

He chuckled. "Likely. But for now, I see mostly benefits in befriending that family. There will always be fear of rejection for the rest of your life. Have faith that this is what you need now. The future will take care of itself. Some of us have a destiny mapped out for us. Who knows? Maybe they can help you interpret and face the dreams. The world is full of possibilities, my child. Stop running and embrace them like all those books you read. Become the adventure. Break free. The only one who believes you should be perfect is you. I want to see the potential inside you blossom. That's my wish and two cents. The choice is yours."

He placed her omelet and grapefruit in front of her. She ate in silence mulling over everything he'd said. Was he right? Had she become afraid to live at all? Always skulking in the shadows of her mind and only projecting what others wanted. What kind of life would she create if she hid from it?

Adam and Alyssa could be her ticket to learn more about the world and be an active participant. She didn't want to be permanently benched on the sidelines. A deep craving for excitement and wonder pushed her to consider new possibilities. Although, it could destroy everything she'd built here. Maybe the time to break the mold could wait. After graduation she could try new things.

What to do? What to do?

She started making the pro-con list in her head while she helped clean up the kitchen. He gave her time to think in silence. After they finished, she cleared her mind and helped him in his workshop. She loved the smell of fresh wood chips and sawdust. The scent reminded her of him every time. He loved creating unique pieces of furniture for all their family members. She enjoyed watching it all come together, especially the ones he made for her. She didn't have his talent to create beautiful masterpieces, but she admired them.

The zip of the saw and scratch of the sandpaper brought her peace. She never doubted that she was loved here. Her papa and grandmother had given her the perfect home away from home. She belonged. Her truest sanctuary wasn't a place. That honor belonged to her loving grandparents—especially her papa. His patience and understanding were unsurpassed.

Monday morning came too fast. Kate had stayed with her grandparents all weekend and felt recharged. Random thoughts from the last week whirled around her mind, and she couldn't handle any more fights with her mom.

She still hadn't made a decision about the twins. Trust was the hardest part for her to move past. Alyssa made her laugh and Adam stirred something inside her that she worked hard to avoid. Romantic entanglements never ended well for her. Boys had too many urges and she couldn't block all the thoughts. With Adam, could it be different? Alyssa and her mom seem so comfortable with all the strange stuff in their lives and in hers. Maybe they had been sent for her. Was it possible her endless prayers had been answered?

Doing the only thing that made sense, she ran and hid in the library. She couldn't make up her mind. No matter how many lists she created, a clear decision wasn't there. Or maybe it was and she didn't want to accept it. She skipped lunch to avoid Adam and Alyssa. She needed a place to think. Sinking into her favorite sofa, she let her mind drift over all the possibilities.

"Kate, what are you doing?" Adam's deep voice jarred her. "I thought we were past the running away thing."

She took a deep breath to control her racing heart. He had the uncanny ability to sneak up on her, and she didn't like it. "Obviously, I'm sitting in my chair in the library. Peacefully, until you showed up. Do you have to follow me everywhere?"

"Don't think so highly of yourself." He smirked at her narrowed gaze. "After sparring and dinner the other night, I thought you'd gotten the disappearing out of your system. You didn't respond to any of my text messages this weekend."

His accusatory glance rubbed her the wrong way. She hadn't agreed to anything specific. "Look, maybe you're right. I'm still skittish today. Had a long weekend and my mind is all over the place. On top of that, I'm not sure it's safe to talk here. Last week, I felt like someone was watching me. It creeped me out. So, I haven't processed everything, and I need to if I'm going to move forward. Things have to make sense."

He shifted his feet and wouldn't meet her eyes. "That might be my fault."

"How?"

"When you ran that first day we met, I didn't know if you could be trusted. I followed you here. When I want, I can pretty much stay invisible. I watched you sort through the information and even find a book to help you understand. I realized you were special. You intrigued me. It's me that you've been feeling here. I've watched you every day because I didn't know how to approach you. I'm not the best with social interaction. Ask Alyssa. She's usually the buffer. Sorry if I caused you any fear."

He looked sincere, and it gave her comfort to know this place could continue to be a safe haven. With the exception of the twins. She didn't know what to do about them. *What the heck?* She needed friends and they seemed to need her, too.

She stood and looped her arm through his, then smiled. "It's okay. I never sensed any danger. Just be honest next time and tell me you're here."

"Done. Can I invite Alyssa to join us? She won't give me peace until I ask." The affection in his tone spoke volumes. Sometimes, she wished for a sibling. Someone to always stand beside her.

"Of course."

Alyssa must have been waiting outside the doors because it took a matter of seconds for her to come bounding up the stairs. She dropped into the smaller seat beside her. Adam scooted Kate over to share the over-sized chair. It hadn't been built for two.

Her nerves went berserk. She struggled to keep the serene look on her face and calm note in her voice. "Are the two of you always this bold making new friends?"

Laughter bounced off the walls as Alyssa's singsong voice responded. "No, it's very rare to meet others like us. We must seem a little on the crazy side. But we usually only find one or two people like us wherever we move. Our dad does work for the military, and our mom is part of some kind of secret society, along with our aunt. It's the one thing she doesn't tell us much about. She says it's for our protection. And theirs. We've seen enough to back off and not ask questions. She shares what she can."

Kate tried to process the new information. Their parents were like spies. Her mother would have a heart attack. "And you always find others like us?"

Adam cleared his throat and glanced around the library. "We haven't met anyone quite like you," he said in a much lower tone, "but others have gifts. Over time, we began a club and extended it to wherever we moved. It's called *Crusaders for Justice*."

Oh no. She'd nearly been sucked in again, and then they threw something new at her. They had a club called Crusaders? Really? Judging by the look on Alyssa's face, she must've let her mask slip and the expression in its place probably wasn't friendly. The farther she tried to walk away from weird, the closer it pulled her in.

Adam bumped her shoulder. "Don't panic, Blondie. We decided to help others and use the gifts we've been given. Our family has preached serving other people since we were old enough to talk. In each new town, we find like-minded teenagers and do a little sleuthing."

"An example?" Part of her wanted to run again, but where?

"Like finding a lost pet or searching for misplaced items like jewelry. Sometimes, we were simply a friend to someone in need. Nothing crazy like your mind is probably conjuring. We did good. We want to do the same thing here. What do you say?"

Kate still hadn't decided on being friends, and now they wanted her to join a *secret club* using their abilities. Seemed a little much. "I don't know. I'm not going to call myself a crusader, but I've always wanted to help others. I don't know if I have enough control. My family is rooted here until they die, and I don't want to cause them any more embarrassment."

Nodding, Adam took her hand. It sent tingles up her spine. She tried to ignore how much she liked the way he used his thumb to stroke across her fingers. "We get it. Pick a new name. It doesn't matter to us. We can start small. Things we'd probably try to do anyway. Each of us can pick a way to help someone we know. Then, we'll write it on a slip of paper, place it in a bowl, and draw. Once we complete all three tasks, we can decide if this is something we want to pursue or make more challenging."

Seemed reasonable, which is why she doubted it would turn out well. But she didn't see any harm in helping others. Maybe she'd find her calling or stumble upon the meaning of her dream. Her current methods weren't working. "I'll try. If we must have a name, I'm leaning toward, *Protectors of the Innocent*. Sounds like a worthy cause and fitting name for what you described."

"I like it." Alyssa got up and began to pace, talking about symbols and creating an emblem for them. Excessive, but Kate didn't want to drag down her enthusiasm.

Adam ignored Alyssa's chatter. "We need to start small and see what we're capable of accomplishing together. We've learned from past mistakes that it's important." He and Alyssa shared a look that let Kate know all their experiences hadn't been good.

What kind of mistakes? How bad could it be? Alyssa's pacing made Kate's anxiety escalate. "Where do we start?" She focused on Adam. He appeared to be the leader type.

"Something easy to accomplish that won't require a ton of our abilities. We can work up to more. Something that will allow us to build trust in ourselves and each other. Here, let's split up this piece of paper. Write down one person you'd like to help or bring happiness to."

A hundred possibilities flowed through Kate's mind, but she couldn't decide what to write down. The blank white paper mocked her efforts. She couldn't target anyone in her family. They'd freak out and think she'd gone crazy. Focusing back on school, she remembered seeing her friend, Kenzie, who always had a smile on her face, crying in the park last weekend when she'd been out walking. She had never seen her unhappy, but hadn't interrupted. Maybe she could cheer her up or fix whatever had made her upset.

Satisfied, she wrote the details on her portion of paper and dropped it into the candy bowl that Adam had emptied for them to use. Adam and Alyssa hadn't put anything in yet, so, at least, they were having issues finding the right person, too.

Once they all placed their papers in the bowl, Adam swirled them around. "We will number the pieces as we draw them. Then, we'll solve each in that order. Agreed?"

Everyone nodded.

"Number one. Must be Alyssa's. Rescue neighbor's cat." He drew a one on it and set it aside.

He didn't seem surprised, but must have understood the unanswered question in Kate's expression. "Our neighbor lost her cat. They have a strong bond. Alyssa can communicate with animals, so she wants to reunite them. We already have an idea where the cat may be which makes it a good deed to start us off."

Alyssa shook the bowl. "What's next? We're almost out of time before the bell."

He unfolded the next one. "Find out what's wrong with Kenzie and help her find peace and happiness. That's sweet, Kate."

Shrugging, she explained. "I've known her for years and have never seen her sad a single day in her life. Her mind is full of light and love. Lately, a dark cloud of sadness surrounds her. I'd like to help."

"Perfect. Let's draw the last one." He opened it.

Even though it was his, he read it aloud. "Help Tommy fight back against the bully torturing him after school. He's a good kid, a freshman. This senior jerk has been hounding him every day, especially after school. I've intervened several times, but I'd like to help him find a more permanent solution, if we can."

"So, not a guarded escort every day?"

"Not if we can avoid it. He needs to find the courage within himself." Adam ducked his head and busied himself picking up the papers. He avoided her eyes like he'd been embarrassed by his choice.

Kate had never been the type to sit back. If she was going to do this, she'd at least pretend to be in control. "Alyssa, gather information so we can start working on yours soon. I'll make an extra effort to speak with Kenzie and get all the details. Adam, while we are concocting our elaborate scheme for Tommy, maybe you can take him home after school this week and watch over him."

They all agreed to the plan and decided to meet daily in the library. She often brought her lunch anyway and this would also help ease her from using so much energy to create barriers in the lunchroom.

Maybe this year won't be so bad after all. She smiled. *I finally feel like I have a direction in my life.*

CHAPTER 4

"What did you find out, Alyssa?" Kate sat down in her usual favorite library chair. Exhaustion made her feel like she weighed a thousand pounds.

"You look a little rough around the edges today. Something going on?" Alyssa ate her lunch rapidly before Adam could swipe any of it. He had a massive appetite and ate any food left behind or left on the table too long. It gave Kate a few moments to collect her thoughts.

On rare occasions she had her dream twice in one night. Once creeped her out enough but twice was extremely freaky. In the back of her mind, she knew it held significance for her future but couldn't figure it out. She wasn't ready to share it with her new friends either. Gathering her courage, she decided to ask if they had any insight in general.

"I'm alright. Had some intense dreams that wouldn't let me sleep. Ever had anything like that?" Kate crossed her fingers that they provided an answer she could live with.

Adam stayed quiet and wrapped a supportive arm around her shoulder. She liked the closeness.

"Sure," Alyssa answered. "Mom says they're two types of dreams for people like us. One represents unfinished business or clues to what you're solving in your awake state. The second is more like having a vision. It's a sign of something to come or a predestined path."

Kate thought it over, and it didn't sound too bad. "How do you know the difference?"

"Our mom's the expert on that. Whenever you feel like sharing, she's great at interpreting dreams. From my experience, the first type only happens a couple of times for the issue you're trying to solve. The second could last for months until you receive the message. I overheard my aunt say once that she knew a girl plagued by the same dream for years. It seems pretty complicated. Mom and Aunt Jill promised to train me after graduation, so I can be more helpful."

Great. I'm never gonna get rid of this crap. She'd be willing to bet hers fell in the second category, but they were much more intense than what Alyssa had described. Maybe she should work up the nerve to ask Linda to help interpret them. Then she'd, hopefully, finally be free.

Changing the subject before they questioned her sanity, Kate focused on Alyssa's comment about training. "Will you go to college or do you have a different type of training?"

"No traditional college for me. I'll go to school, but it's a specific training center to build my unique abilities. My mom and aunt both graduated from there. I'm expected to do the same. I've seen the school in my dreams and know it's my destiny. It's exciting and scary all at once as we move closer to senior year."

Must be nice. Alyssa had a clear path while she had freaky dreams involving a strange man. She turned to Adam and nearly collided with his face. Her stomach flipped and she felt an insane urge to kiss him. *I must be losing my mind. I'm at school.*

She regained some distance. He smothered a laugh, so he could probably sense her struggle. She shot him a dark look to squash the amusement. "What are your after-high-school plans, Adam?"

"My dad's part of a secret militant society. Most of them have some type of special gift. They use them to help people all over the world. He never talks about the actual cases, but he saves lives. They have a hidden training unit somewhere in South America. As soon as we graduate, I'll join them. According to Dad, with my skill level, my placement will probably be deep undercover. Our parents agreed to no more moves until after we're done with high school. I think they wanted us to have some stability before we answer our higher calling. So you're stuck with us at least three years, and you might find your destiny intersects with one of ours." He brushed her cheek, and she sucked in a quick breath.

Kate wished she hadn't asked. She definitely wasn't ready to map out the rest of her life and devote it to the unknown. They seemed so sure of themselves. Doubts plagued her night and day. Three years would take forever and a lot of things could change. She didn't know why they'd been brought into her life, but Papa believed they could be her guide or help build her self-confidence. At least, she had time to figure things out.

Right now, they needed to get back to the task at hand before the bell rang. "Thanks for helping me shake off the bad night. Alyssa, what can you tell us about the missing cat?" Words she never thought she'd utter.

"Ms. Miller is our neighbor. A really sweet elderly lady. She's owned Sandy, the cat, for ten years. She rescued her as a kitten, and they have a strong bond. Ms. Miller's daughter died a few years ago, so all she has left is a horrific granddaughter who's in her early twenties. She lives down by the river in one of those dilapidated houses. All her money goes to bad habits, if you catch my drift. When she runs out of money, she visits her grandmother and demands cash. Last time, she stole some of Ms. Miller's valuables and pawned them. So, Ms. Miller changed the locks and placed a restraining order against her. I forgot to mention during that last visit, she told the poor lady if she didn't pay up, then she'd take the cat until she paid. Or she'd kill it. Like I said, nasty piece of work."

"But she didn't take the cat that day. So, what happened to make you think she has Sandy?"

"About a week ago, the horrid woman came back demanding more money but she couldn't get in the house. She screamed everything from outside. Ms. Miller called the cops and she was dragged away. She promised to get back at her. Within the next few days, Sandy disappeared. It didn't look like a break in, but Adam was able to catch traces of the crazy girl's scent. That leads me to believe she made good on her promise and took the cat. My guess is she thought as soon as the cat disappeared, Ms. Miller would be calling to offer her money. Why she didn't demand a ransom, I don't know. Maybe she didn't want the cops to think the complaint was real or she figured that she'd already given her an amount the last time she created a scene for more money. Mom told the poor lady to hold off on calling her to give us time. But she won't wait much longer."

And what were they supposed to do about it? Kate thought this would be climbing a tree or tracking the cat down in the nearby woods. Visiting a crazy person didn't feel like a good idea. "How do you propose we rescue the cat?"

Moving their lunch bags off the table, she laid out a schedule that had been color-coded. "I've been monitoring her movements for a few days. I've figured out the perfect time to sneak in and take the cat back."

"You want us to break in?"

"I don't think we'll have to. Sandy knows me, so we shouldn't have to be in the house long. Plus, these are abandoned homes that were damaged in that storm y'all had several years ago and aren't owned by anyone except the city. Dad said they declared the area a flood plain. The city will probably tear them down soon and try to find a developer to create something in the space. You know, something that makes money."

Kate loved reading mystery novels but hadn't intended on becoming a sleuth herself. She had no doubt Adam and Alyssa came from a family of doers. Her parents believed you should let the police do their job. Would they rescue a cat? Probably not. Danger signs lit up inside her head. She'd met Ms. Miller in the grocery store a few times. She'd always been so nice and didn't deserve this.

Her internal radar of justice outweighed any misgivings. It wouldn't be a big deal. "When do you think we should do it?"

"After school today. Ms. Miller is ready to offer a lot of money and Mom is out of reasons to hold off. Who knows if the idiot is even feeding or mistreating Sandy? I don't think waiting is an option. We drove and can take you home or to the studio when we finish." Alyssa's demeanor had shifted to one that meant business. The giggling girl disappeared. Kate wasn't the only one hiding behind masks. She couldn't ignore the change in Adam either. He resembled a trained soldier ready to attack.

What had she gotten herself into? If they considered this small scale, she didn't want to imagine what they'd done in previous locations. The problem she'd dropped into the bowl seemed ridiculous now.

"I usually have tutoring after school on Thursdays, but Wes is out sick today. My mom isn't expecting me home until dinner. I'm good to go." Kate hoped she didn't live to regret those words.

When the bell rang, they agreed to head directly to the car after school. Alyssa hurried along, but Adam hung back. "Hey Kate, I wanted to ask you to see a movie with me tomorrow night. Actually, *us*. Alyssa will be there, too. I didn't want to make you uncomfortable or rush you. One other thing before you answer… Would it be okay if I held your hand in the hallways or put my arm around you? I've seen how you like personal space and I don't want to intrude."

She froze, trying to formulate the right response. She didn't know if she was ready to go in that direction, but they couldn't stay still either. She couldn't deny the attraction. Her mother wouldn't allow dating until she turned sixteen, but this might be a way to test the waters. "Yes, and yes. A movie sounds fun and gets me out of the house. My mom has a lot of rules about dating, but as long as Alyssa is with us, it should be fine. And hand-holding I'm okay with, but not a fan of any deeper public displays."

"I'm good with that." He smirked and took her hand. "Besides, who said anything about PDA? Your mind must be in the gutter."

She aimed an annoyed glare in his direction. Laughing, they entered the last class of the day.

The teacher drug on forever. Anticipation charged every cell in Kate's body. She'd always loved detective shows and mysteries. Supernatural shows were also a guilty pleasure that her mom would freak out over. Maybe that's why she watched. Most of them were about catching the bad guys, too. She had an insane desire for justice she couldn't explain. It had been a part of her since birth. Papa always told her that she'd been hard-wired to protect her fellow man. Now, she could test that theory.

They hurried to the car and tossed their backpacks in the trunk. On their way to the south side of town, they remained silent. No one wanted to add tension or cast doubts on what they were doing. Kate's mom would be giving her a lecture on falling in with the wrong crowd. She'd call them busybodies and say they were looking for trouble. She refused to admit her mother's voice in her head had merit.

"Almost there." Alyssa turned on the right blinker and pulled down a gravel road.

Most of the houses were barely standing. A few years ago, some severe storms had crashed through the town. The people in this area hadn't been able to rebuild, so most of the homes had been condemned. Over time, several squatters had taken shelter in them.

They stopped behind a treed area so no one would notice. *Not like anyone paid attention around here.* A short thin woman with long matted hair pulled back in a ponytail stumbled out to her car.

"That's her. She works at the bar down the street. Don't know how she stays employed. I guess they're desperate for help. When she pulls out of sight, we'll head to her house. Look, she left the front door open. I consider that an invitation."

Kate still considered it a private residence of sorts. However, they should probably make sure everything was okay and lock up the place. Being a good citizen was important. And she'd keep telling herself that until they were safe.

"Let's go." Adam had scoped out the house to make sure they didn't encounter any surprises. "Stick to the tree line, blend in with the surroundings. I didn't notice anyone home nearby, but better to be safe. We'll quickly enter the front door and locate the cat."

Slowly, they made their way to the entrance. Kate kept looking over her shoulder, waiting to be caught any second. The cloak and dagger routine seemed a little much. They entered the doorway. She kept her mental radar active the whole time. So far, no one had seen them.

The house resembled a war zone. Broken furniture, rotting food, and dirty clothes spread out over every square inch. And the wretched smell of urine, vomit, and all things foul had her gagging. "Alyssa hurry up and find the dang cat. I can't take this." Adam didn't seem to notice or maybe he had the ability to turn off his sense of smell. She wished she did.

A hiss came from behind a door. She dreaded what they would find. Adam opened it and Alyssa moved in quickly. She gasped and bent down to the cat. It hissed again and bared its teeth. The fur had mats of blood, and the poor cat probably hadn't eaten in days. Burns were also evident beneath the fur. Sandy had been tortured. The redness around the injuries could be infection. She didn't blame the cat for being testy, but they needed to get out of here.

Adam stepped back where he could watch the front door. She noticed neither of them had touched anything. She didn't plan to either. She didn't want the plague.

Alyssa dropped to her knees despite the feral cries for her to back off. She whispered softly, and the cat began to calm down. Then, she lowered her head and locked gazes with Sandy. They were silent, but Kate could see Alyssa's aura expanding. She didn't want to intrude on her thoughts but sensed they were communicating.

After a moment, Sandy moved forward and allowed Alyssa to pick her up. She held her in a blanket and tried to avoid touching the wounded areas. Tears flowed down Alyssa's cheeks. It dawned on Kate that she didn't just share thoughts. She could feel Sandy's pain and emotions. She had a brand new respect for her friend.

A rattling sound caught her attention. Adam pushed them back away from the door. "A car is coming."

Kate opened her mind to connect. "It's the crazy girl. She remembered leaving the door open and doesn't want the cat to escape. She planned to kill Sandy tonight and deliver her to her grandmother because she still won't give her money. Her thoughts are all over the place. She's certifiable. We need to get out of here. *Now.*"

"There's a hall closet at the back. You can tell she never uses it. We can hide in there until she leaves." He pushed them toward the back. Then he opened the door and shoved them inside. "Alyssa make sure the cat knows not to make a sound."

The girl entered and went straight to the room where she'd hidden the cat. Once she realized it wasn't there, she emitted a horrifying howl. This lady needed to be locked in a straitjacket. She tore through the room and then moved to the next one. Every kitchen cabinet made a loud bang as she threw them open one by one.

They stayed as still as possible. Alyssa whispered. "She's not giving up. Her thoughts are scattered. Eventually, she'll open this door. We don't need that kind of confrontation. We'll end up in trouble or worse. What do we do? I don't think she can see reason at this point."

Taking a deep breath, Kate focused on the gift she usually kept locked away tight. "But her mind is susceptible." Closing her eyes, she connected with the insanity raging in the woman's head. She blocked the erratic thoughts and instead projected the compulsion to leave immediately and return to work. She reinforced that she'd lose her job if she didn't leave now, and then she'd have no money for the partying she wanted to do later.

Standing up, the girl went to the front door. She hesitated, so Kate sent another push. The door shutting rattled the walls of the house. She stayed connected to make sure she didn't have any second thoughts to return. Once she entered the main highway, Kate disconnected and leaned back against Adam. Using and maintaining that kind of mental energy always exhausted her.

He placed his arm around her and supported her to the car. They exited and disappeared into the tree line. Once they got to the car, everyone gave a huge sigh of relief.

"I didn't plan for that much excitement." Alyssa placed the cat into the carrier, then shifted the car into drive. She peeled out of the lot. "Kate, what did you do? I've never seen anything like that. My mom has mentioned compulsion but it's super rare, especially in someone your age. But I'm glad you can. It just saved us."

To save them, she'd revealed one of her deepest secrets. She didn't want anyone to know she could command the mind. This whole charade didn't seem like such a good idea anymore.

Adam held her tight against him. His strength transferred into her, restoring some of the drain. "Sorry, Kate. I never meant to put you in this position." He kissed the side of her head.

Alyssa moved through the streets but made sure not to speed. "We need to get Sandy to Ms. Miller. Then, I'll drive them both to the vet. She'll probably have to stay the night. I'll ask Mom to help with protecting the house in case the freak-show woman returns."

"She won't." Kate still had her eyes closed.

"The lady seemed pretty determined to find the cat. Why wouldn't she?"

"I stripped her memory of using the cat for revenge. Or more like I buried it. Her mind is too scattered to figure it out. They should be safe." She snuggled closer to Adam, letting his warmth wash over her. She should probably push him away, but it felt nice to lean on someone else for once.

"You can do that?"

Adam kicked the back of Alyssa's seat, warning her to stop asking questions.

Kate pretended not to hear by faking sleep. She'd better not reveal anything else. She'd already blown their minds. Adam didn't seem to care, especially when Alyssa told him he'd have to drive Kate home.

When they arrived at Ms. Miller's, she cried for fifteen minutes and thanked them profusely. All the doubts bouncing around Kate's head came to a halt. She let the emotions of the lady surround her. They'd done a good thing and helped a deserving person. Her cat was the only thing left in the sweet lady's life to fight her loneliness within.

Alyssa had been right. They could make a real difference, if she had the courage.

This time when Adam dropped her off, he kissed her cheek. They were moving forward, but should they be? What if they started a relationship and then broke up? It would destroy the friendship, and she'd probably lose Alyssa, too.

He must have sensed her internal doubts. "Stop worrying so much. We'll always be friends first. I promise you that. But don't give up on something that could be great because of fear. Who knows where our adult lives will lead us? Let's enjoy the one we have now."

Made sense. She put her arms around his waist. A bold move for her. "I'll hold you to that promise. See you tomorrow." She hugged tight, then went inside.

Luckily, her mom had gone to visit her sister, so the house was quiet. She grabbed one of her favorite books and let all the stress of the day drift away. In her books, she could do anything and be anywhere.

"I feel guilty now," Kate said. "Ms. Miller and Sandy were an excellent example of helping others—*innocents*. Mine seems a little weak." She met with Adam and Alyssa in the library the next day to debrief.

"Remember, mine wasn't supposed to be difficult," Alyssa said, casually filing her nails. "Pick up a cat. Go home. I'm happy yours is less dangerous. Helping others comes in all shapes and sizes. If your friend is hurting, then let's help her. Have you been able to talk to her?"

Kate took a seat beside Adam. "I talked to her briefly this morning," she responded. "We're getting together tomorrow afternoon at a coffee place. I'll figure it all out. I know it has to do with her boyfriend, Sean. I can't help feeling they have a strong connection every time I see them together." Adam kept playing with her hair, making it very hard to focus. She couldn't wait for the movie tonight.

"I'll find out a little more on Sean this weekend," he said. "I've gotten the same vibe from the two of them. We get to play a little cupid." The bell rang and he pulled her up from the sofa, forcing her to crash into him.

He smiled and whispered in her ear. "I'm hoping Cupid pays us a visit, too." He laced their fingers and they headed to class. A new routine she'd become fond of.

Her mother had to work late, so Kate managed to avoid that part of the drama. Papa had brought her home from karate training to get ready. He fully encouraged the friendship and left before they arrived. But he did say that he wanted to meet them both soon. Adam and Alyssa pulled up at five-thirty. They grabbed a quick bite to eat. None of them wanted to pay for the expensive movie theater food.

Adam tried to pay for her meal, but she wasn't ready for that yet. She paid for her own movie ticket too. Too many years of her parents warning her to be careful that there was always a price for kindness created a strong sense of caution within her. She wanted to stand on her own two feet and not depend on others. Silly, but she couldn't shake it. She was afraid that pride might, one day, be her downfall.

She had to give Adam credit. He didn't say a word, just smiled and squeezed her hand. They found seats in the center and shared a popcorn while the credits ran. Once the movie started, Adam placed his arm around her and tugged her slightly toward him. Her first instinct was to break free. Instead, she relaxed and laid her head on his shoulder. Alyssa sat on her other side. From the outside, they probably appeared as close friends. Kate wanted to believe it could be true. Once again, her mother's warnings came to mind about people using her to gain control of her abilities. What were they really after?

"Stop, Kate," Adam leaned over and whispered. "Fear is taking hold inside you. Take a chance. You won't regret it."

Somewhere deep inside, she couldn't shake the feeling that pain was inevitable. She'd seen them both do so much good, and their family had given their entire lives to serving others. They could teach her a lot. Even if they only showed her the way to freedom and the opportunity to find her purpose, it would impact her life forever. Her mother's caution and Papa's encouragement waged a war inside her mind. Tired of all the doubts, she locked it away in her *worry about it later* compartment. For now, she wanted to enjoy the movie with friends and her time with Adam.

Once she cleared all that clutter, her feelings toward Adam started to surface. His patience unnerved her. He exuded strength and confidence. He'd made his own way in this world and didn't doubt the course of his future. She wanted that kind of clarity. She wanted him even though she valiantly fought the building desire. It wasn't simply an attraction, but everything he represented. He and Alyssa could help her discover the internal persona she'd bottled up so tightly out of desperation to fit in.

Being heavily attracted to him happened to be a huge bonus. If this worked out, she might gain a best friend *and* a boyfriend. Maybe guardian angels were more than a myth, and hers had sent what she needed most before she'd driven herself crazy. She'd still keep the world at arm's length, but her mind and heart began to find balance.

After the movie, Adam dropped off Alyssa first.

Kate hugged her. "Thanks for not giving up on me. I'm not the easiest person in the world to get along with."

"That's the definition of friends. It's a requirement to put up with the crazy along with the insanity. Your abilities are wicked. Don't be afraid of them or us. You don't have to thank us. That's what friends are for." A fact she'd finally begun to understand. Before she knew it, they were sitting in her driveway once again.

Now for the hard part. He'd told her a few days ago that, when she was ready, she only had to ask. *Here goes nothing.* "Adam, I know I've been hesitant about the whole boyfriend thing. To be honest, I've never let any boy that close because I couldn't handle the backlash of emotions. With you it's different, but I'm still cautious about how this will work. Long story short, I'd like to try being your girlfriend, if you'll give me time to figure this out along the way."

Waiting the few seconds for him to respond was brutal. "That's what *I* want, Kate. I'm not in a rush. Baby steps. I thought it'd take a year to get this far, and it's only been a few weeks. Miracles happen." He laughed as she punched his shoulder.

He cupped her cheek and her stomach flipped. She couldn't hide the hint of fear. "Never be afraid of me, Kate. Baby steps, remember?" He leaned forward and brushed his lips across hers.

All sorts of strange feelings warmed her entire body. What would happen when he decided to deepen the kiss? It felt like playing with fire yet, like a moth, she was drawn to the flame. She floated out of the car in a daze. It took everything she had to leave him behind and walk inside. Part of her wanted to explore the new emotions raging inside. Her parents were watching TV, so after a quick exchange of hellos, she headed back to her room without being interrogated. She laid back in her bed and let the daydreams of happily ever after flow. For the first time in her life, she actually believed it could happen.

CHAPTER 5

"I can't believe fall break is only a couple weeks away. This year is flying by." Kate tossed her backpack on the ground beside the picnic bench. They'd decided to take advantage of the warm sunny day and eat outside.

Adam squeezed in beside her while Alyssa sat across from them and began asking questions about their next mission. "Where are we with Kenzie and Sean?" She used hushed tones.

Good question. Kate wished she had a better answer. They had fallen behind on their grand plan, due to life and homework getting in the way. Things had gotten much worse between Kenzie and Sean. "It doesn't make sense. I can feel it clearly that they want to be together, but something has caused a massive amount of damage. Neither trusts the other one."

"Did one of them cheat?" Alyssa asked.

"I don't think so," Adam said. "I've spent time talking with Sean. Kate's right. Something else is happening. He's hurting from the loss of the relationship and a feeling of betrayal."

"So is she," Kate added. "I'd only admit this to you two, but I went against my own number one rule and pried into her thoughts. Sean has accused her of stealing some of his mother's jewelry, which she didn't. I searched thoroughly for that. She's maintained her innocence and he wants to believe her but can't move past the doubts. It happened during dinner at his house a few weeks ago. Sean, Kenzie, and his mother were the only three in the house at the time. I can see why it's hard for him to see an alternative. It doesn't help that his mother is also suspicious and wants him to stop seeing her."

They cleaned up their table and headed back to the library for full privacy. Alyssa paced, sorting the information. "Maybe we're looking at this the wrong way. We don't need to simply get them back together. We need to catch the thief and return everything to normal. Hearts will heal when truth is revealed. One of mom's favorite sayings."

"Makes sense, but, once again, sounds like we might be getting in over our heads." Kate tended to be a visual person, so she pulled the mobile whiteboard to their area and grabbed a few markers. On one side she listed facts. On the other side, she wrote theories and clues. "What we know is the date and time. We also know who was in the house. We believe them all to be innocent. Where does that leave us? A lot of people would steal for money, but I feel it's something more."

"Maybe." Adam stared intently at the board, then reached for the marker. "It has to be someone who knows their routines, what kind of jewelry the mother owns, and where she keeps it hidden. That narrows the suspects to only a few. I doubt she goes around broadcasting where she hides her valuables. I'm guessing it had to be someone they trusted at some point. I did a little mental digging of my own with Sean. His mother is a widower and doesn't date, so nothing there."

After writing down all the information, they had to go to class. Kate rolled the whiteboard into the storage room. No one went in there, except her. "We need to gather more facts from Sean's past. When I looked through Kenzie's thoughts, I picked up on some threats from an old girlfriend. It's a place to start. Adam, see if you can get Sean to open up some more, especially about his ex. We could be way off base, but we could, at least, rule her out."

Alyssa came to a dead stop. "Wait. What about Tommy? Should we take care of him first?"

Shaking her head, Kate motioned for her to move forward. "It turns out our grandmothers are good friends. My grandmother and I convinced his family that the after-school Taekwondo program that I used to attend would be perfect for him. He'll learn skills that he needs in order to protect himself and it buys us time to create a lasting solution. The program picks him up from school and his mom grabs him from the studio. Once he's attained a little training, I think we can do more for him and empower him to create his own solution with our assistance."

Adam pulled her in close and kissed her cheek. "You're amazing, Kate. That's perfect. I'll work with him on the afternoons I go to the studio. Brilliant. Everything's working out."

On the surface, it seemed that way. Kate still had her doubts. They were definitely meddling and, at times, overstepping personal boundaries. She'd invaded a friend's thoughts and would probably do so again. They'd found answers, but at what cost? She'd bet anything Adam would do the same with Sean. Where should the line be drawn? Did the ends justify the means? She didn't know, but it bothered her constantly.

The next few days became a blur. She spent more time than usual finding out everything she could from Kenzie. The ex-girlfriend had become more of a nuisance than she'd first realized. Didn't make her a thief. But it did move her up their list of suspects. So far, she hadn't found any reason for the girl, Clara, to need money. However, revenge or jealousy was always a good motive. Kenzie pointed her out in the hallway.

Time to get to know the enemy.

Instead, Clara found *her* after first block in the girls' bathroom. Kate could take her down easily but decided to play along, acting startled. She also sent a message to Alyssa for back up. She couldn't have planned it better if she'd tried.

The girl snarled. "What were you and that skank looking at me for? You got something to say? I dare you." Her eyes gleamed with rage. This one had some mental issues.

Kate fought the urge to smack her. She needed information. "I believe the skank you refer to is my friend, Kenzie. I assure you she doesn't deserve the title. However, from the stories I've heard about you, well…" Her eyes narrowed and Kate smothered a laugh. So easy to bait. Alyssa had slipped in unnoticed and hid in the corner.

"I've taught that witch a lesson, so be careful or I'll teach you one, too. My daddy has a lot of power in this town, and I'll make sure he destroys you. It wouldn't take much, would it? I've heard all the rumors about you." Her fake sweet smile made Kate's stomach turn.

She fought the fear rising inside. She wouldn't let this piece of trash get the better of her. "Go ahead, spread your lies, but I brought my own insurance policy." She pointed to Alyssa in the back, who held up her phone like she'd been recording everything. "Wonder how daddy would like this spreading around town? If I'm not mistaken, it's an election year."

The aura surrounding Clara turned to swirling shades of red and black full of violence and anger. It masked the fear held deep inside, but she couldn't hide from Kate. Clara had a secret, and she aimed to find it.

Kate connected to her mind and searched her memories. She'd been relentless in her sabotage of Kenzie. Her thoughts were dangerous and disturbing. Finally, Kate found what she'd been looking for. The memory of Clara sneaking into Sean's house while they were eating dinner came into focus. She crept up to the mother's bedroom. At some point, while they were dating, she'd followed his mom to her bedroom and discovered the hidden panel in the back of the closet. She opened it and swiped the jewelry.

She took it home and hid it in her room under the bed. The pieces of jewelry had become trophies for what she believed to be her success in dividing the happy couple. She didn't want Sean back, but she didn't want Kenzie to have him either. Her punishment for both of them.

Disconnecting, Kate met her eyes. Clara huffed and stormed out of the bathroom. Alyssa ran over and hugged her. "Did you get what you needed?" Kate nodded. "Then let's head out. Adam is climbing the walls outside."

They didn't want to wait until the next day, so they went to a local restaurant and picked a back table to avoid eavesdropping. Kate quickly filled them in.

"So, we know the thief. At least our sleuthing chart worked. Good to know for the future. But what now? We can't go into their house like we did the crazy granddaughter's. They'll be locked up tight and have lots of video cameras." Alyssa tapped her fork against the counter until Adam jerked it out of her hand.

"I don't know." Kate pretended to eat but mostly pushed the food around her plate. "We can't let Kenzie take the fall for that witch, but we also can't call the cops because we'd have to explain how we know the information. That leaves us where?"

Her whole body clenched in frustration. She wanted Clara to pay for all the pain she'd inflicted. The only way for that to happen would be if she came clean and admitted what she'd done, or if she panicked and gave herself away. Why would she do that?

She met Adam's gaze and a slow grin started to form. "You thinkin' what I am?"

"What are you two planning?" Alyssa glared from one to the other. "This can't be good. So naturally, I want in."

"Let's take this to the car. It's getting a little crowded in here." Adam paid for the meal, and they left. They'd begun taking turns paying for meals, so it worked out for all of them.

Once settled in the car, Adam drove until they reached a remote area, then he pulled over. "To answer your question, we were thinking Clara needs to be spooked. If she believes someone is on to her, then she might move the jewelry or try to sell it. Either way, we can be ready and have Sean catch her in the act. Kate, we'll need Kenzie to be the catalyst because she has the biggest ax to grind. Do you think you can convince her?"

"Of course, I can. One way or another. Although, I don't think it will be that hard. I just need a plausible story on why I know. I'll think of something. One of you will have to lure Sean to the right place and time, and it would help if we had a police officer in the right spot, too." Kate racked her brain, trying to figure out who had connections. Then, it hit her.

"Wes, the guy I tutor. His older brother works for the city police force. I can use Wes to convey the message of something he's overheard at school. His brother is new and looking to make a name. I'm pretty sure he'll follow up, even if it's just a possibility."

"Excellent. This is coming together. We can solve two problems at one time. A theft and a relationship. Mom will be very proud." Alyssa seemed genuinely happy. She had parents who would pat her on the back and say, *well done*. All Kate had was a mother who'd condemn her for getting involved and tell her how stupid she'd been. She envied their freedom to be who they were born to be. Living in the shadows, hiding behind her masks had become lonely. She'd always believed it was the only way to live, but what if it wasn't?

She arrived home ten minutes before curfew, avoiding a lengthy interrogation. She'd meet with Kenzie tomorrow during lunch and plant the confrontation. Adam would make sure Sean overheard and felt the impulse to follow Clara. Kate would pass all the day's drama onto Wes and plant the suggestion to tell his brother. A lot of moving pieces would need to fall perfectly into place.

Nausea overwhelmed her. What had she gotten herself into? She wasn't some teenage sleuth from the novels she loved. She'd spent years controlling her surroundings and protecting others from her gifts. Now, she'd begun using them at will, manipulating others into doing what she asked. A slippery slope. If she saved lives and helped others find happiness, did it exonerate her?

Guess I'll find out soon enough.

She'd already made plans to stay at her grandparents' this weekend to have a little more freedom and to avoid walking on eggshells. Closing her eyes, she accepted the dream that would surely come and the fear of what it meant.

"What are you staring at ho's?" Clara's winning attitude never ceased to amaze. Kenzie and Kate had waited for her in a hallway outside the cafeteria.

Kenzie started to freeze, so Kate mentally hit her with a heavy dose of courage. This wasn't her fight. She nudged Kenzie to respond. "Not much at all. I'd say you're about to be finished."

Clara jerked her head and crossed her arms. "What does that mean? You don't scare me."

"Maybe I should, once I tell the cops all I know."

"Which is what, airhead? No one's gonna believe a word you say anyway." She sent them her best drop-dead glare and acted bored.

Kate stayed connected to both of their thoughts to maintain control and avoid surprises. This needed to go smoothly to work. Clara hadn't caught Kenzie's drift yet, so she placed a hand on Kenzie's back to remind her why they were here. She continued providing Kenzie the confidence to continue. Sweat rolled down her back. She hoped this confrontation didn't take too long or they'd be picking her up off the floor.

"That night at Sean's, I saw you climbing outside the window and thought you were just a jealous wench, but then his mom's jewelry went missing. I know it was you." Kenzie stepped forward no longer needing Kate's assistance.

"You're just trying to pass the blame off on me cause he dropped you. Don't worry, I don't want anything that's been with you." A little fear started to form in Clara's mind, but she maintained her hateful expression.

"Nice try, but after Sean accused me, I went back to look around the house and found one of your cheerleading ribbons on the ground." Kate had given Kenzie that information after discovering in Clara's mind that she'd lost it.

"If that's true, why wait so long? I think you're full of crap and desperate to hang on to that loser, Sean." Once Kenzie mentioned the hair ribbon, the hint of fear grew exponentially in Clara's mind.

Kate encouraged Kenzie to keep up the pressure. "Honestly, I wanted Sean to figure it out for himself, but that hasn't happened, and I have nothing else to lose. I'm not going down for your desperate act for attention. I recorded our last several conversations, so I'm showing that to the cops too. I'm also giving it to Principal Stevens and turning you in for bullying."

"You wouldn't dare." Clara's eyes narrowed and for a second Kate was afraid she'd lash out.

"Try me." They stood nose to nose. Kenzie didn't back down. Her hands were in fists at her sides. "In fact, I plan to go tomorrow and you'll be finished. Enjoy your last minutes of popularity because I intend to take it all away. Everyone will know who you really are and how you torture others."

"Don't threaten me you cheap piece of trash. My daddy will destroy your family and you'll be forced to leave this town and your precious band geeks." Clara's face turned bright red and she started to stammer.

"We'll see about that. Time has run out on your charmed life. Tick. Tock." Kenzie taunted as Clara spun on her heel and ran off.

When they finally made it back to the library, Kate could barely stand. She'd never used that much mental energy in her life. The conversation with Kenzie had been pretty easy but getting her to act on it had taken a lot more than she'd planned. Kenzie tended to be reserved and non-confrontational when outside of her band crowd. Having her confront Clara took an enormous amount of compulsion. Then, controlling the situation had added more strain.

Adam helped her sit down and relax. She asked about his part of the plan. "How did it go with Sean?"

"I made sure Sean overheard the conversation but prevented him from intervening. I didn't think I was going to be able to hold him back for a minute. His guilt is something fierce. Instead, I convinced him that Clara needed to be followed if he wanted any chance of obtaining his mother's prized possessions and to clear Kenzie's name."

"What about you, Alyssa, any issues?" Kate tried to keep her eyes open.

"Nah. Just a bunch o' prissy airheads that were way too easy to distract. A pain in my butt but didn't take much brain power. I kept anyone else from overhearing or interrupting. All in all, I'd say we were pretty successful." Alyssa brought her a coke and some candy to build her strength back. Everyone had played their part and now they had to cross their fingers and hope for the best.

Adam pulled Kate against him and kissed her cheek. "Do you have enough left in you to convince Wes this afternoon?"

"I should. It usually doesn't take long to recover." *Unless I'm changing someone's natural state of thinking, like convincing them to do something completely out of character.* She'd keep that to herself. "Wes is easy going and genuinely will want to help his brother. He's a big gossip so that helps, too. His brother always picks him up because they are sharing a car right now. I'll pass on some reinforcement to follow his instincts. I think that's all it'll take." Hopefully.

She forced down the dread building inside her.

Alyssa reached for her hand. "This will work, Kate. Don't be such a worry wart. Together we can handle anything." Kate wished she had the same confidence.

She gripped Adam's hand tight and made it back to the library for her tutoring session. Her palms were sweaty and her heart raced. She took several deep breaths to steady her mind.

"You got this," he leaned over and whispered. "I'll be upstairs in our spot if you need anything. Once this is over, I think it's time for a date with just the two of us. Think about it. We can find a way." He gave her a quick embrace and headed upstairs before Wes walked in.

"Hey Kate, I've got a Chem test on Monday and need a good grade."

She slid her mask into place and motioned him to sit. Time to become the perfect friend and teacher he needed her to be.

"So, he bought it?" Alyssa turned around in her seat and asked Kate for a second time.

"Yes, he even mentioned his brother needed to know without me suggesting it. I added extra encouragement into the mix. I think he'll show. Clara's mind is still leaning toward taking the items to her grandmother's. They have a hidden safe, so she thinks they'll be protected until all this blows over. We need to catch her before she enters the house. They have to be in her possession for this to work."

Kate had already cleared everything with her mom, who thought they were all going out to dinner. She'd promised to be home early. Tucking in behind some other cars on the street, they watched as Clara waved good-bye to her dad. He usually had late-night meetings, leaving Clara unsupervised most of the time. Her mother hadn't appeared in recent memories, so Kate assumed she'd died or left many years ago.

The moment her dad drove out of sight, Clara ran into the house. A few minutes later, she emerged with a small pouch tucked under her arm.

Alyssa pointed at the purse. "That's it."

"How do you know what's in there?" Kate agreed with the probability, but Alyssa didn't have any doubt.

"You have your abilities, and I have mine. The jewelry is in there. It matches the description Adam pulled from Sean. All we have to do is follow without being seen." She sent Adam a pointed glare.

He returned it with one of his own. "I know what I'm doing, Sis. Sit tight. This is my area of expertise."

Kate enjoyed their banter and it gave her further insight into their abilities and training. Tracking, investigating, and questioning seemed to be second-nature to them. Their parents had taught them to be self-reliant and highly skilled. It also made her appreciate her own mom a little more for giving her a normal childhood instead of preparation for combat or Armageddon. Both ways had merit.

As predicted, fifteen minutes later they approached Clara's grandparents' home. She cast furtive glances all around her. Adam motioned toward the trees where he'd instructed Sean to hide. Kate sent the compulsion for him to confront his old girlfriend.

"Clara, why did you take my mother's jewelry? You know what they mean to her? I trusted you."

She spun around to face him. "I don't know what you're talking about," she spluttered. "What did she say to you?"

"Who? No one told me anything. I overheard part of your conversation with Kenzie today. I followed you, hoping to prove you innocent. I never thought you'd stoop so low. And you did it to break up my relationship. You dumped me, so why are you determined to cause us pain? Give my mother's stuff back. *Now.*"

Kate had never considered Sean as menacing until this moment.

Clara hesitated then tightened her grip. "I don't know what you're talking about. I'm just returning something to my grandmother, and you're *crazy*. Leave now or I'm calling the cops."

Indecision crossed his face, but he didn't back down.

"No need to call the cops, miss." Wes's brother stepped up from the side yard. "Tell me what's going on here."

Sean pointed. "She stole my mother's jewelry and won't give it back."

"I did not. I'm *returning* something. I already told him that."

All the commotion brought out her grandparents who demanded to know what was happening. The officer informed them of the accusation and asked to see the pouch.

Clara's grandmother started to refuse, but Kate reached out and urged her to investigate. She couldn't do much from this distance but it worked. "I tell you what, young man. Describe the items you think are in the bag. I'll lay them out."

She took the bag from Clara's hand, and Sean showed her several pictures from his phone. Then Wes's brother confirmed them from the police report. While dumping the items onto the hood of the car, she gasped. Everything matched. The look on the elderly lady's face sparked terror in her granddaughter. These weren't people who tolerated a scandal.

"Due to the value of the stolen items, I have to place her under arrest." The officer's expression hardened but Kate also caught his excitement to make a collar.

"Of course, I'll call her father and our family lawyer." She turned to Clara. "Wipe that smirk off your face, young lady. You're not getting out of this. How dare you bring shame into this family? Go with the officer."

Clara's head dropped as the weight of her actions fully sank in. She began sobbing when the officer placed her in the back of the police car. Kate hoped this would teach her a lesson and put her back on the right path.

Sean walked over to their car and leaned through the window. "Thank you. I'm not sure how or why you were able to figure all this out. I'll never be able to repay you. I'm heading to Kenzie's to beg forgiveness—not that I deserve it. I should have trusted her and looked for another explanation. Kenzie knew it was Clara, but I couldn't see it."

"Tell her that, Sean." Kate reached out and patted his arm. "Tell her what you just told us. Let her know how you feel. Begin to rebuild trust, and I think everything is going to work out just fine. I expect to see the two of you at lunch tomorrow."

Chuckling, he nodded. "Yes, ma'am." He ran to his car and sped off.

A sense of rightness washed over her like something in the universe had been corrected. How odd. These two were perfectly matched and, despite their young age, would stay together. She couldn't explain why she knew that, but she did. If soulmates were real, they were a shining example. Comforting and terrifying all at once to feel this much.

Adam dropped her off at home and reminded her they needed to plan something soon. She agreed and went inside. She'd arrived home early as promised, but could tell from the moment she entered the kitchen, her mom wanted a confrontation.

"Where have you been?"

Uh oh. Kate steeled herself for the inevitable. "Out with Adam and Alyssa as I told you."

"And what were y'all doing?"

What on earth had bit her mother's butt tonight? "We ate dinner and then went to the park for a little while. What's going on? Why are you looking for a fight?"

"Wes Turner's mom gave me a call tonight and wanted me to thank you for giving his big brother, Jim, a heads up for some kind of arrest. So, I turned on the news and guess what I see. A teenager caught for theft. She goes to your school! What did you do?" Her mother's enraged gaze didn't falter.

She should've thought of that minor complication. "Look, I didn't do anything crazy. I overheard my friend, Kenzie, and the girl who got arrested arguing outside the cafeteria. It didn't take any special skills to put it all together. While Wes and I were working on chemistry, he mentioned his brother struggling to fit in at work. I gave him the information to pass along. Did you see me on the news or in any way connected?"

A clock ticked in the background, grating on Kate's nerves. Her mother depended on logic, and she'd given her facts—or at least the modified version. She started to take a peek in her mom's mind but figured that wouldn't help. She'd learned a long time ago it was best not to venture there.

"Fine, Kate. Sounds reasonable enough. But remember, you have to stay out of things in this town. No one ever forgets. If anyone suspects you could be used to catch people or solve crimes, you'd never have a moment's peace. I know you don't want to listen. And I'll even admit that there's this piece inside you calling for justice." Her mother smiled at her stunned expression.

"I know you more than you give me credit for, sweetheart. There are a lot of people who will use you with the best of intentions, but will create the worst of consequences. You're reaching an age where my power is limited. The weight of responsibility is shifting to your shoulders. It breaks my heart to say this, but you know I plan to live out my days in this town. I won't let you destroy that for me or our family. Just as you need your space to grow, I need mine to live and survive. I love you, Cadence. I always will, and I'll admit I'm not the best at showing how deep my love is. But I'm beginning to understand your future path will take you away from mine." Her mom's voice broke and tears flowed down her cheeks. "I will have to make my peace with that and keep you safe for the few years I have left."

Kate had gotten her wish to be understood, but it felt awful. Even with all her efforts to protect her family, she'd still managed to disappoint. The weight her mother referred to would eventually bury her if she didn't find a way to deal with it.

Her mother walked away with her head held high. She'd said her piece and would never mention it again, as was her custom. Three years until graduation seemed like forever but in the back of her mind, Kate knew time would move swiftly, and she'd soon say goodbye. It left more sadness in her heart than she had expected.

Resisting the urge to call Papa, Kate went into the guest room beside her bedroom. She'd turned it into a practice studio and had even convinced her stepdad to hang a punching bag. He never contradicted her mother, but provided her support where he could as long as he didn't have to get too close. He possessed the fear that she would read all his innermost thoughts. Like she wanted in his head. Yuck! She cleared her mind and used her patterns to wash away the emotions of the day.

Happiness for helping friends.

Sadness for being a disappointment to her mother.

Kate swept it all away.

The smell of sweat caused her nose to crinkle. She'd been working for over an hour. The solid movements and predictability had brought her peace. She switched to the punching bag, using every combination imaginable, until all her muscles screamed out in protest. Then, she headed to the shower.

Warm water washed the rest of the day away. Her thoughts turned to Adam and what their next date should be. They'd have to include Alyssa for a while, especially with her mom already suspicious. Maybe another movie. She'd ask tomorrow. Excitement and anticipation filled her. Her feelings for him continued to grow. Even though she wasn't ready to label them yet, she also couldn't deny the emotions were taking on a life of their own.

CHAPTER 6

"Tommy, I can't believe how much you've progressed in the last month." Kate had convinced her master instructor to fast-track him. He'd earned two belt advancements in the last month and she had him ready to test again in the next few weeks.

"I know, right." His excitement overflowed.

She and Adam had made sure to push but not overwhelm. His confidence level had increased exponentially. It tended to fade during school, but here he felt that he could conquer the world. Soon, he'd have to confront his bully and move forward. Because of his natural talent, she hoped he'd continue the program.

He hung around longer than usual after class. "Tommy, is there something else?"

"Well." He shifted from side to side. "There's this girl I'd like to ask to the masquerade ball next month, and I was sort of hoping you might help me out. I don't have a clue what to say."

"Of course. You can point her out on Monday. We'll come up with a great plan, and Adam can help with the words, too. Okay?"

He beamed and hugged her. "Thanks, Kate. Thanks, Adam."

She expected him to run off, but he didn't. "Something else?"

"A silly question, but I've been wondering for a while, and I'm just a geek about stuff like this. I know your name is Cadence. I see it all over the studio. It starts with a 'C'. But when you write Kate, you use a 'K'. I was wondering if there was any significance in the letter change."

Laughing, she pulled him up from the mats and headed toward the dressing room area. "I'm afraid there's not much mystery there. When I was little and determined to shorten my name, my mother insisted on using a C. My obstinance demanded a K to make my own mark on the world. Eventually, I won, and now everyone uses the K. If you notice, even my current Taekwondo awards use the name Kate. I think you're the first person to notice or ask me about it. You have a great inquisitive mind. Never lose that." She ushered him into the boy's locker room, so she could head to the girl's room and get changed. She had plans to meet up with Adam and Alyssa tonight to watch a movie.

Over the last month, it'd become their routine. On Tuesdays and Thursdays, she ate dinner at Linda's. Mondays and Wednesdays were her nights to eat with her parents. Friday nights, she, Adam, and Alyssa did movie and dinner. She'd become a creature of habit and loved every minute of it. Most weekends she spent with her grandparents.

She and Adam continued to circle around their relationship. They were together, yet not quite. He still hadn't deepened the intimacy with their goodnight kisses. Part of her was ready to move forward and part still wanted the safety net. They'd have to make a decision soon. Maybe it'd be easier once he met Papa.

Tomorrow night her friends would be meeting her grandparents, who had insisted on being introduced to Adam and Alyssa. Adam seemed excited to meet her family and Alyssa always wanted to get to know new people. Kate had gone to great lengths to keep them far from her mother. Around her, they'd have to watch every word out of their mouths, but it would be much more relaxed with her grandparents.

Kate cleaned up and dressed quickly. Adam believed Tommy had reached a point he could face his bully, Cody. After today's practice, she agreed. She wanted to complete this mission they'd started weeks ago. She hated unfinished business. They'd still have to help and provide him with a little extra knowledge and confidence. They'd agreed to lay out their plan over dinner.

He still ended each night with a quick kiss on the cheek or a soft brush across her lips. She could tell he wanted more, but she always hesitated and he'd immediately step back. He never pushed or acted disappointed. She wanted to trust him completely and let him into her heart, but she couldn't forget her mother's words of caution and feared he was using her for her skills. She was pretty sure he wouldn't wait forever. Too many girls already followed him around drooling. He'd be incredibly hurt if he could read all the doubt in her mind, so she kept it locked away.

Building up the courage to talk to him should be simple, but so far, she'd chickened out every time. She rushed out to their car and Adam sat in the backseat with her, while Alyssa complained she felt like a chauffeur. Adam laced his fingers with hers and gave her that lopsided grin she'd grown very fond of. Butterflies fluttered rampantly in her stomach. Her heart skipped a beat. All these crazy feelings had to mean something. How had he become so important in her life so fast?

He snuggled her against him until they were thigh to thigh. "Mom packed us a food basket since it's actually warm today. The weather is very strange here. Thirties one day. Seventies the next. The park will give us more privacy. She also sent a blanket for when the temperature drops."

Right now, Kate's internal temperature was approaching combustion level. Adam drew circles with his thumb on the back of her hand. Maybe he wanted to torture her or remind her what she was missing out on.

Alyssa drove into an isolated but well-lit section of the park. "Here we are boys and girls. I vote we eat first. That way, if it gets too cold, we can talk in the car."

"Sounds good to me." Kate already felt a chill in the air. It helped cool her overheated body.

It didn't take long for them to eat and decide to return to the car. When the sun faded, so did all the warmth. They piled back in the car and huddled under the blankets to avoid wasting gas. The quicker they had a plan, the sooner they could head to the movie and indoor heat.

Trying to stop her teeth from chattering, Kate listened while Adam laid out all the details. "Cody is a senior and has decided to make every day of Tommy's life absolute misery. I did some asking around, expecting to hear how big of jerk Cody is to others. Instead, he seems to be a great guy, until you mention Tommy. So after some digging, I discovered that Tommy's dad is a financial advisor. Cody's dad had a lot of investments with him including Cody's college fund. After a couple really bad investments, he lost a lot of money including the college fund. From what I can tell, Tommy's dad warned him against the investments. But Cody's dad insisted trying to maximize a payout to afford the Ivy League school Cody wants to attend. When Cody found out the money was gone, his dad passed the blame onto Tommy's dad. That's why he has so much animosity."

"How do we fix that? Even if Tommy wins the fight, it won't solve the bigger issues." Kate shivered.

Adam pulled the blanket over her shoulders. "I talked to Dad, and he has a computer expert who helps on some of his cases. He's tracking down the documents to prove what happened and the emails showing that Tommy's dad warned him against the investments. Then, Cody and his father can have an honest conversation and figure out what to do with their future. First, I think we need to let Tommy and Cody face off physically. After, we can give Cody the folder with the information. My guess is there won't be any further issues."

Alyssa drummed her fingers on the seat. "So, why have the fight at all? Give Cody the information and end it."

"He's too far gone to listen to reason. I've been watching him, and he's convinced his friends that Tommy is evil. For this to be over and done, Tommy needs to make a stand with our assistance." Adam turned to Kate. "One of my abilities allows me to transfer knowledge to another person. I can't move it permanently yet, but it lasts for a couple of hours. I figure between the two of us, we can give Tommy what he needs, without lasting effects."

Doubts clouded Kate's mind. She wasn't too sure about sharing her mind, and she'd have to hide many things behind strong barricades to protect herself. There were some things she never intended anyone to know. "Why do you need me? You have plenty of skill."

"But you're a natural warrior and see everything around you. That's what he needs. I can't give him that, and I promise not to look beyond your boundaries and will share only what you allow. I won't push. I open the channel, and you push the information. My role is a conduit. It only lasts an hour or two at best, so we have to be careful with our timing. To be completely honest, it will create a stronger mental bond between us. That part will be permanent, so you have to be willing to take the risk." He watched her as she sorted through the information.

She didn't know what to do. Her mind had a full-scale war debating whether she should or shouldn't. Tommy's face came into view and she remembered his haunted expression when they'd first met. He'd learned so much over the past few weeks and deserved the chance to prove himself. Pushing the fear aside, she nodded her agreement. Adam would either earn her trust or break her heart. Either way, she'd survive and would help a friend in need along the way.

"Ok, so let's lay this out before we become popsicles and miss the movie." Adam took charge. "Alyssa, you need to draw Cody to the spot and let him know Tommy will be there. Once everything is in motion, your job is crowd control. We don't want any permanent record of this. Kate, you and I will follow behind Tommy. We'll give him space to stand up to Cody, but be there to assist. I'm thinking Cody will bring backup. They'll try to jump in. We'll be there to provide an even playing field."

"So now we're looking for a fight too? My mom's going to kill me if I'm caught mixed up in this." *What have I gotten myself into?* Kate tried to hide the panic building inside.

"No. We're there to protect Tommy from others joining the fight. Hopefully, we won't be involved at all. However, I like to be prepared." Adam's eyes narrowed.

His soldier mentality frightened her at times. She wasn't tough and fearless like them. Her mom had already made it clear that she didn't want any controversy. This could go very, very wrong.

Pulling into the parking spot, Alyssa turned. "My addition is this. We tell Tommy about the issue with Cody and their dads. He deserves to enter the situation with all the knowledge. It's his choice how the battle must be won. We only provide the opportunity and protection if necessary. Kate's right, Adam. Never forget the boundaries. Mom and Dad have always been clear on that."

It was the first time Kate had heard such command in her voice. She seemed fun-loving and laid-back but possessed a core of steel just like her brother. She wondered if their younger siblings would be the same. Maybe someday she'd ask. For now, she'd stick to the task at hand. "When do we set this in motion?"

"Tomorrow morning."

"Tomorrow? Are you crazy, Adam? We just devised the plan."

He pulled her from the car and tucked her against him. Her breath caught in her throat. "Oh, ye of little faith. Most of our kind are still sleeping on Saturday mornings, so it won't draw as much attention. Cody and his pack of friends just entered the theater, so it'll be easy for Alyssa to slip the information. I've already texted Tommy and asked him to meet me an hour before. The less time he has to panic, the better. Everything's falling into place."

Sure, until a piece falls and shatters into a billion pieces. They entered the movie and selected their usual seats. She couldn't concentrate on a thing. She tried to catch enough to answer her mother's usual questions. Feeling unprepared had her on edge. She didn't like walking into loaded situations and this seemed like a prime example of just that. Who knew what Cody could be capable of? What if he brought a weapon?

They were going to be in so much trouble.

The morning frost bit Kate's cheeks, and her fingers tingled. She'd worn her favorite black athletic pants and blue fitted top. She wanted freedom to move if she had to fight. Before leaving the house, she'd thrown on a hoodie for warmth.

Wish I'd remembered to grab gloves. Her mom had left early to go shopping with her sister, so there'd been no parental confrontation. Hopefully, it'd stay that way.

"Morning." Adam and Tommy walked over.

"Where's Alyssa?"

"She's already setting everything in motion and leading Cody to us. Tommy, we'll be behind those trees right there." Adam pointed over his shoulder. "Call out if you need us. No one will enter the fight except you two. Are you sure you're ready?"

Adam's concern sounded genuine but excitement also radiated in his eyes. Kate tried to control her own erratic nerves.

Tommy hesitated. "Yes, but I'm not sure if fighting is the answer. I know I need to end this or I'll never be free. He has friends in all four grade levels. I guess I'm a little afraid."

"You should be. That's normal." Kate stretched her arm around him. "But I promise you're going to have the courage and wisdom to see this through. Do you trust me?"

He grinned. "Absolutely."

"Go into the clearing and wait." Tommy followed her instructions, and she turned to Adam. "How do we do this? I want to make sure he's prepared."

"He'll have your guidance. How could he fail?" He kissed her cheek, and she glared.

Reaching for her hand, Adam faced her. She opened her mind and connected through their telepathic link. She'd spent a lot of time last night hiding most memories and thoughts in her mental compartments, but left knowledge of karate and the skills gained from her master instructor open to Adam. She transferred them like she projected her thoughts, and he functioned like a switchboard and placed the knowledge inside Tommy through a mental link.

Tommy wasn't prewired to be a telepath, so it took a lot of effort from Adam. The strain to maintain a forced connection could be intense, which is why she avoided it. Kate watched as Tommy's confidence grew. His eyes glazed over momentarily, then he had laser-sharp focus and awareness. His intensity reminded her of herself.

Scary thought.

She pulled Adam behind the tree. A cold sweat had broken out across his face. He used his jacket to wipe it off and took several deep breaths to recover from the exertion. One thing she'd learned is that there was always a cost to the mental stuff. She should take that as a warning to stay away from it.

"Hey, *punk*." Cody broke through the bushes and approached Tommy. "It's time for us to settle a little score."

"I have no score to settle with you." Wow, Tommy sounded just like her.

Cody sneered. "I say, we do. I brought a few friends to help me get the point across."

Alyssa had already given them a heads up that several had come with the intention of getting a shot at Tommy. It made her sick that people could be this stupid and cruel. She and Adam stepped out of the trees and moved in front of the angry mob, trying to join Cody.

Adam held out his hand and motioned them to stop. "This is between Cody and Tommy. If any of you step forward or try to intervene, Kate and I will stop you."

"A girl? You brought a girl to the fight. How sad are you, man?" One of the idiots smirked in her direction.

Kate smiled and met his gaze. "Don't you remember me?"

Panic crossed his face. "Oh, shit. You're the crazy one that can make people blurt out the truth." He ran away before she could respond.

"Guess he had secrets he wanted to keep. How about the rest of you?" They had a moment of indecision, but advanced.

She moved into her fighting stance. "Wrong answer."

The first boy threw an errant punch, which she easily avoided and followed with an elbow to the back. Sweeping his legs, she took him to the ground. Adam had pulled two in his direction, so she focused on the next one giving her the eye.

He had a few more skills. He aimed several kicks toward her head. She deflected and landed a spinning side kick in his midsection. He hopped up quicker than the last one. He attacked from the front, while another joined the fight from behind.

If they couldn't fight fair, she'd teach them a lesson. She sent an open-hand palm strike into the face of the one in front of her. Then, she reared her head backward to hit the head of the one behind her. They'd have black eyes for sure. Not showing mercy, she sent three front kicks into the chest of the first. Switching to back kicks, she delivered the same amount to the second assailant.

Once they picked themselves off the ground, they ran. She wiped their memory of faces and names as they fled. She wouldn't risk them spreading rumors. Adam finished off his two, and she completed the same memory adjustment. She and Adam stood back to back and motioned for any others to make their move. After a few moments of sneering and hesitation, they all went home with modified memories of the day.

With all the extras out of the way, Kate and Adam returned their attention to Tommy. Kate looked at Cody. "If you feel this must end in a fight, then so be it. But if you choose to cheat in any way, you answer to us. Do you understand?"

He nodded. Anger dominated his persona and created an ugly twisted look on his face. He lunged at Tommy who easily sidestepped the attack. When that failed, he tried barreling in like a linebacker. Tommy waited and used pressure when Cody leaned down, taking him off balance.

Cody fell to the ground, scraping his hands and knees. Kate scanned him quickly to make sure he didn't have hidden weapons. She found that his rage had increased to the point of insanity. Cody lunged again. Tommy clocked him square in the jaw.

Howling in pain, Cody threw wild punches and kicks. Tommy deflected them all. He swept Cody's legs, then straddled his chest. Without proper skill, Cody wouldn't be able to escape. Tommy had him pinned.

She waited for Tommy to force him into submitting. Instead, he reached over and grabbed the file folder Alyssa had given him earlier. He held it over Cody's face. "This contains the truth of your precious trust fund. It has all the emails between our dads. Just so you know, my dad has worked day and night to rebuild this money for you. Not because he did any-thing wrong, but because he's a good man who wanted to help. He's better than all of us."

Cody still struggled, but began to listen with a little dose of calm from Kate.

Tommy spoke from the heart. "I took karate lessons to face you today, I think it's obvious I could have beaten you severely. But fighting doesn't solve anything. It only destroys lives. Read what's in the file. Then, if you want to finish this, name the place and time. I'll be there. All I ask is you read this first. Please?"

Kate held her breath. Would it work? He'd used one of her master instructor's favorite weapons. Use your words, not ac-tions, to find a resolution. He taught them to only fight when it was necessary to save your life or someone else's. Finding a peaceful option took much more skill than throwing punches. That lesson had been the turning point for her mental control. She'd harnessed her anger and found absolution.

Tommy moved off Cody and held out his hand to help him up. He grabbed the folder from the ground and went to a nearby table. It didn't take long and his head dropped as the truth hit full force. Instead of walking away, Tommy sat down beside him. Kate, Adam, and Alyssa stayed in the background.

Cody wiped his eyes. "My own dad lost my college money. It's all I ever wanted. My ticket out of this small, stupid town. It's gone."

"Maybe not. Your dad loves you and sold off some of his as-sets to let my dad invest them the right way. It's not as much, but it's a start. You'll be able to go. I believe my dad will help you. I'm guessing your dad blamed mine to save face. Maybe it's time to clear the air with him and begin a new plan for your future. Getting busted for fighting won't help either of us."

"I'm sorry, Tommy. I know that doesn't make up for how I've treated you all this time or what I tried to do today. I became obsessed with making you feel the same pain as me. The moment I started reading my dad's words, sanity finally returned."

He turned and faced them. "I'm sorry to you, too, and thank you for intervening. We all needed to learn a lesson today. You could have set me up and had me arrested. But you didn't."

Alyssa moved to his other side. "We didn't want anyone to be in trouble. We wanted you to find peace and move forward. You can now." Her soothing tones relaxed the tension in his shoulders. His eyes still held sorrow but not shame. She had an amazing way with people and emotions. "Go home. Your future is what you make it."

Tommy and Cody headed home, while Kate dropped into the car. Exhausted.

She picked herself up and leaned forward. "We completed all three. I'm ready for a break."

"I'm ready for dinner. Isn't it at your grandparents' place?" Adam rubbed his stomach like he hadn't eaten for a week.

"Real subtle, Adam." Alyssa took a long drink from her soda bottle. "It's barely lunchtime. What are we going to do for the next few hours? I need sleep."

"Why don't we head on over to their house?" Kate said. "Papa knows what we've been doing and will understand if we need to crash for a bit. Then, we can help fix dinner and have a relaxing meal. Remember, Papa is open to all topics, but my grandmother is more reserved on some things. When dinner is over, he'll invite us to his workshop. We can talk freely there." Kate leaned back against the seat, trying to stay awake.

Alyssa started the car and backed out quickly. "Sounds good to me. I need to recharge, and *soon*."

She turned out onto the main road. Kate's next coherent thought reminded her that someone from today could talk or have a video. "Hey Alyssa, what about cell phone pics or videos?

"We're good. Mom gave me this awesome device that prevents phones from working. They scramble and are hard to even turn on. Between that and your memory boost, we'll be fine. Plus, I don't think Cody wants any of this getting out."

She had a point. Kate gestured to her left. "Turn here, and it's about a mile up the road."

"Thank goodness. I thought I'd have to pull over for a nap first."

Papa didn't question. He motioned them into the living room and let them sleep off the day's events.

Dinner had been fantastic. Both her grandparents adored Adam and Alyssa. Her grandmother had even winked and pointed at Adam. Subtlety had never been her strong suit. They all helped clear the table and wash dishes. When her grandmother settled in to watch her favorite TV show, Papa motioned them out to his workshop.

"Wow. You guys have had quite an impressive day." Papa sat back in his chair after hearing all the details. "I'm happy to see my Katie has good friends accepting of her abilities. She's never been able to share a bond like that before. I try, but don't have the skills she needs. Only a willing ear to listen, I'm afraid."

"That's more than enough." Kate leaned over and hugged him. "Always has been."

He cleared his throat. "Now that you've solved the big three, what's next?"

They looked at each other, unsure.

"We know we can help others accomplish any task," Adam finally answered. "I guess we'll continue to work with each other to assist those in need, while improving our abilities along the way. I'm hoping something comes along soon. I like helping others. Our parents say that's the highest calling one possesses."

"I think your parents are correct, young man. I'm certain, when the time is right, your next challenge will present itself. In the meantime, it's almost Thanksgiving and that means time for the annual Masquerade Ball. Will all of you be going?" He asked so innocently, but Kate knew what he was after.

It appeared Adam did too. "Yes, we all plan to attend. We hear it can't be missed. I had planned to ask Kate to be my date, but I understand her mom doesn't allow dating. So, I guess we'll go as friends."

"Hogwash. I'll take care of her mother. Besides, I'll be there. I help with the electrical work each year. That old mansion has many issues. I can supervise." He used air quotes for the last bit and winked.

"In that case…" Adam stood and reached for her hand. "Kate, will you be my date for the Masquerade Ball?"

She grinned. "Absolutely."

CHAPTER 7

"What about this one?" Alyssa twirled around the dressing room.

Kate shrugged. "I don't know. The color's great, but the shorter style doesn't suit you." She flipped through several dresses and grabbed ones with potential. "Try these."

Turning back to the fitting room, Alysa looked over her shoulder. "What's the deal with this dance anyway? The whole town's buzzing about it. I've heard of proms but never a winter formal this important."

"Supposedly, the founder of the town came from wealth but wanted to make his mark on the world. He came here. He built businesses, a school, a bank, and even a library. Back then, advertising wasn't easy, so he created a masquerade ball and sent invitations to all neighboring towns and to his home country. He planned and prepared for months, aligning the date with the winter solstice."

"But why do all that? He'd already built the town." Alyssa stepped out again. They both shook their heads, and she motioned for Kate to continue while she tried the next one.

"He had a town, but not a lot of people. He wanted it to grow and prosper, which meant he needed town citizens. Anyway, the story goes that people from all over came to the ball. They were so stunned by the beauty and grandeur that they decided to stay and make this town their home. In addition, the man met his future bride that night. It's said that she stood at the bottom of the stairs and the moonlight blessed her. Even though he couldn't see her face behind the mask, he fell instantly in love. I'm sure a lot of that has been romanticized over the years.

"It became a town tradition to celebrate growth and success as well as a way to find true love through matchmaking efforts. This lasted for generations. The significance eventually faded. About fifty years ago, the town decided to bring back the celebration to remind everyone of our history and to inspire them to seek true love or, at least, enlightenment. Everyone pitches in to clean up the mansion and decorate it to perfection. I went last year to check it out. Pretty impressive and definitely had a strong vibe. You'll love it." Kate thumbed through her selection of dresses while she waited. They'd agreed to take turns, so they could find the perfect gown for each of them.

"I think this is it." Alyssa squealed and stepped out. She reminded Kate of a regal princess. The red gown had a fitted bodice and a bottom which fell in layers that swirled slightly as she walked. She'd found the perfect dress. Kate hoped she'd be that lucky. Her nerves were still on edge since accepting Adam's offer to attend the dance with him.

Twirling, Alyssa grinned at Kate. "I swear this was made for me. Now, it's your turn." She ushered Kate into the tiny dressing room. "No buts. Get in there. Besides I want you to look decent if you're dating my brother. We've got standards, you know."

She ignored Kate's glare and dropped onto the nearby sofa. "All joking aside, I'm happy for you and Adam. I know you have a lot of doubts and our futures seem pretty scripted, but one thing I've learned is that fate takes a path all its own. You two are good together. And I'm thrilled to have a great friend. To be honest, I haven't gotten close to anyone before. We've moved so much. When our parents promised to give us some time here and then we met you, I just knew our lives intersected for a reason."

"To drive me crazy?" Kate opened the door.

Alyssa grinned, but crinkled her nose at the dress. "Not that one. Try the blue gown that matches your eyes."

Before she reentered the room, she turned and faced Alyssa. "I have the same feeling about our meeting. I've never allowed myself to have a close friend. Holding everyone at a distance was much easier for me to handle. No matter what happens with Adam, I'm beginning to believe we've created a lasting friendship. You also happen to be right about this dress. Yuck."

"How about this one?" Kate barely contained her excitement. From the moment she pulled on the blue gown, she knew it'd been made for her.

"Amazing. The color changes in the light just like your eyes. It's like a designer created it just for you. Incredible. What are the odds?" Alyssa walked around her and nodded. "Accessory time."

The two of them spent another hour picking out shoes and several other items to complete the ensemble. Kate didn't know how the dance itself would turn out, but she'd look great.

Adam had borrowed the car to run errands for his dad, so Alyssa's mom had offered to do drop off and pick up detail. They still had an hour before she'd arrive. Motioning toward the food court, Alyssa suggested they grab some lunch.

The past few weeks, she, Adam, and Alyssa had continued to find small ways to help others. None had created quite the adventures of the original three. Maybe those had been some sort of cosmic test or to encourage a strong friendship. Either way, she was grateful. Adam had become a little restless and wanted to find something bigger. She liked the anonymity of small tasks.

It'd taken a while to get her mother on board with letting Adam escort her to the dance. The one concession she'd had to make to gain permission required Adam and Alyssa to join her mom and dad for dinner before the ball. So, this weekend might be a complete disaster.

All they had to do was act completely normal and not set off of her mother's inner warning signals. No topic could be considered safe. *On second thought, disaster might be an understatement.*

"What are you worried about, Kate? Your aura gives you away every time."

Kate rolled her eyes. "Lucky for me, no one else can read my aura. As long as my expression stays serene, I'm good."

"Serene, my behind. Don't look in a mirror now, but anyone can see something's upset you." Alyssa's pointed stare nailed her with truth.

"Fine. This dinner with my parents is going to be horrendous, and I don't how to fix it." There, she'd laid her biggest fear out on the table.

"Look, Adam and I know how to handle those who aren't ready to see beyond the boundaries this world has created. I promise we won't say anything outside the ordinary and we'll be careful with every question we answer."

Alyssa's eyes softened and she laid her hand on Kate's arm. "Your mother loves you. She simply can't comprehend all that you are. So, you place everything inside you in this tiny box. You try so hard to be what she considers normal, but I think you're starting to comprehend that your future is going to be unique. The war in your mind and heart is okay. If we didn't question things in this world, where would we all be? Dinner will be great. Focus on the masquerade. The masks we found rock, and we'll be stunning. Everything is as it should be. Trust me."

If only she could let go of the anxiety and trust with her whole heart, Kate's life would be much easier. Linda picked them up and Kate hung out at their house for a while. Alyssa and her mom had found several books for Kate to read about mental abilities. Her mom would have a stroke if she knew what all she'd learned the last few months. But Linda never judged and patiently answered her questions. It'd become clear the family hadn't met anyone with her unique abilities, but they accepted her anyway. They tried to help her and support her. Something she'd never forget.

Adam drove her home. She sensed he had a little anxiety of his own about meeting her parents. Each night he brought her home, he'd lightly kiss her cheek or brush her lips softly before she stepped out of the car. Would the dance change things? Part of her hoped not, but another piece wanted to see what could exist between them. With the dance a couple weeks away, she'd find out soon enough.

"Welcome. Come on in and have a seat. Dinner's almost ready." Kate's mom ushered Adam and Alyssa into the dining room. "Kate didn't tell me much about your preferences, so I hope pot roast, fried potatoes, and green beans will be okay." How had their liking, or not liking, the food become her fault?

Adam slid by her and squeezed her shoulder in support, but Alyssa went right up to her mom and gave her a quick hug. "Sounds perfect, Mrs. Martin."

Her mom placed all the food on the table and nodded for her dad to say the blessing. After everything had been passed around and plates were full, the questions began. Surprisingly, her dad spoke first. "Kate mentioned you're sixteen, Adam. Since you have a car, I assume you work, correct?"

"Yes, sir. I work for my dad. He has a hectic schedule, so I take care of the household, repairs, and I also help him with research and paperwork for his job." Kate held her breath as Adam gave the perfect answer.

"So, what does your father do?" Uh-oh. Maybe not a great answer.

"He's retired military but still does a lot of consultant work. We're both history buffs, so that's where I come in with research. With all the travel, I couldn't hold an outside job. It works well with my school schedule, and I help my family." Adam had this parental information dump down. Even she wanted to commend him for his service.

Satisfied, her dad returned to his meal. Her mom redirected the conversation to Alyssa. "What does your mother do? I understand you have more siblings."

"Yes, ma'am. She works mostly from home. She and my aunt own a research firm. With multiple children, my mom doesn't travel much. My aunt takes care of that aspect. My cousins are grown and away at college. Adam and I help where we can. It's hard to raise two sets of twins, I suppose." Kate began to have a sneaking suspicion that these answers had been cultivated over time. The stories were flawless and neither gave a hint of dishonesty.

In most ways, they were being truthful. No wonder they hadn't feared this dinner. They'd grown up in the shadows telling the world what it needed to hear for them to maintain normal lives. They understood her struggles more than she gave them credit for. Yet, the family valued total honesty with each other. Maybe that's how they found balance.

Her mother's nod hinted at approval, but she wasn't done yet. "I've been hearing a lot of rumors about the three of you galivanting around town and being nosy. Why is that? We've taught Kate to maintain a quiet existence."

Crap. "Mom, that's rude." Even her dad sent her mom a cross look.

Adam tensed and Kate felt his fist clench against her leg.

"My mother would agree it's best to be humble and stay behind the scenes," Alyssa answered without hesitation. "She also taught us to help others and treat them as we want to be. Kate, Adam, and I don't look for trouble. I won't speak for Kate, but Adam and I will assist whoever is in need within reason. Risk and danger are not part of that. I assure you."

Her mom's face flushed from the gentle chiding.

Adam cleared his throat. "I know we're new in her life and to this town. Ask whatever you need to check us out."

The kitchen timer dinged, and Kate jumped out of her chair. "Cookies are done."

"I can hear, Kate. Run and get them since they've excited you so." Her mother laughed and looked at her like she'd gone crazy. Kate didn't want to leave the table but her nerves had gotten the better of her. She'd look ridiculous if she refused. At least her mother had played it off and cracked a joke. A rare occurrence for her.

She threw open the oven and loaded the plate as fast as humanly possible. Alone time with her parents wasn't a good thing, and Adam had opened the door for more questions.

Luckily, when she returned, her dad had engaged Adam in a conversation about rebuilding a Mustang engine and Alyssa had distracted her mother by mentioning the scrapbooks she'd seen lying on the side table. One of her mother's passions, so they became fast friends when Alyssa showed her new easy-to-use techniques.

Awestruck, Kate glanced around the table. She had so much to learn. They'd managed to fit in without using a disguise. Instead, they'd used their talents and wits to handle everything and not have to hide. The power of observation had been their greatest weapon.

The rest of the night progressed without issues. Until the time came for them to leave, and her mom starting asking questions again.

Their escape had been so close. "One thing we didn't get a chance to discuss is your future plans. What do y'all intend to do after graduation?"

A quick glance crossed between the siblings, and Kate held her breath.

"My plan is to join the military," Adam said.

"What branch?"

"I'm not sure yet. I'm still deciding the best fit for me." Kate mulled over his answer and wondered what branch would be considered for that type of highly classified missions.

"I'll attend school after graduation," Alyssa said, "and eventually join the family business."

"Where do you plan to attend?" Her mom wasn't backing down.

"I'm undecided. It's a big world, and I haven't figured it out yet."

"I see. Seems like the two of you have your futures figured out. Kate hasn't yet. She's still struggling to fit into this world at times. I don't want her to be influenced to become some vigilante or philanthropist because those she spends her time with have some misguided concept of what she is or could be. I hope the two of you understand, and I never see that type of behavior around my daughter." Her mother had seen more than she'd given her credit for.

Kate didn't need her mom making veiled threats to the only two real friends she had. She started to speak, but Adam stopped her.

He turned and met her mother's accusing stare. "I understand. Kate is special, and as long as one or the other of us is around, we'll do everything in our power to protect her. But you have to know she'll embark on her own path to discovery. All I can promise is to stay a true friend until the end."

Her mother's eyes watered as the sincerity of the answer overwhelmed her. He'd loaded it with raw emotion and even

Kate teared up a little. "I guess that type of friend is all a mother can ask for. I hope you stay true to that promise, no matter what discoveries are made over time. I'll be watching closely."

"We intend to honor our word." Alyssa's voice held the authoritative note that always sent chills down Kate's spine. It signaled she'd had enough of this show for tonight and didn't like the doubt evident in her mother's tone. They were both ready to escape after only a few hours.

Welcome to my world.

Kate started up the grand entrance stairs but noticed Adam had stayed behind. He stared at her with a look of amazement.

"What is it, Adam?"

"Nothing. It's just... You're so..." He struggled with his words, so she tried to wait patiently.

Taking a deep breath, he stepped closer. "The moonlight has encased your entire body in a golden glow—almost like a spotlight created just for you. Even your hair sparkles, and I swear your eyes are swirling with a dozen shades of blue, lighting up the mask. It's mystical. You look amazing."

"Thank you, but it's only an illusion. I'm the same old me. However, your words were beautiful." Kate took off her mask and held out her hand. He laced their fingers and led her up the staircase.

When they reached the top, he gently tugged her closer. "You're wrong. Everything about you is special. This gown is awe-inspiring in itself, but nothing without you. All you need is a crown and you could be a real princess."

"No royalty here I'm afraid, but I am in the market for a handsome prince. You interested?"

"Oh yeah." His free hand lifted to cup her chin, and he leaned in and placed a soft kiss on her lips. "*Very.*"

Her heart skipped a beat. This had turned into a moment she'd only read about in books. She'd captured his total attention and couldn't be happier. It had become easier to give up and let go of any hope, versus letting someone get so close to her. His eyes shined with emotion. She wasn't ready to label it as love and certainly wouldn't ask him. Nature would take its course and lead them in the right direction. His fascination gave her a boost of confidence. She felt magical tonight.

As they entered the room, everyone turned and stared. She had to give some credit to the gorgeous gown she'd found. The blue, sleeveless, satin bodice had a low cut back and gave way into smooth folds that gently rustled when she walked. She'd found silver sandals with a slight heel, making her feel like Cinderella. In an absolute stroke of luck, she'd found an antique decorative ring and a mask with the same tone of blue, surrounded in gold and silver to make the ensemble complete. She hadn't recognized herself in the mirror.

For once, she didn't mentally alter her appearance for anyone. They moved farther into the room and everyone returned to dancing. The student council had spared no expense to create the perfect mysterious scene. Tables with black linens lined the walls, and the buffet had been placed along the back. The dance area took up the center with polished floors and a grand chandelier. Roses were laid on every table and hung in each entryway. Even the floor had rose petals sprinkled across the width of it. A live ensemble played a waltz. Traditional songs were always played, along with newer selections. Oddly enough, the townspeople had learned the older dances that enhanced the experience.

All her life, Kate had watched from the outside, desperate to be a part, yet terrified at the same time. Adam pulled her into his arms, and they waltzed around the room. She closed her eyes and followed his lead. For a moment, she imagined being a princess just like in the fairy tales she loved. Too bad dreams didn't tend to last. At midnight, would everything disappear?

He twirled her around, and she forgot her worries. Alyssa passed by and laughed. She'd decided to come with Cody. They'd become good friends since she'd begun helping him and his dad work through their financial issues, or more specifically, the emotional impact of them.

"Hey Kate, watch out for your secret admirer. He looks like he's finally worked up the courage to make a move." Alyssa's laughter faded into the crowd.

Kate assumed her reference meant Jimmy had decided to come. He'd tried to get close to her many times over the years. He wasn't bad looking and seemed nice. But he only knew the image she projected, so she'd always turned away his advances.

"Um… Kate, I was wondering if we could dance, if you're free." Jimmy stumbled over his words. She felt bad for him but didn't want to say yes.

"Sorry, man." Adam bailed her out. "Tonight, all her dances belong to me. However, I've seen that Janice keeps your looking your way. You should rush over there and ask *her* to dance."

"Really?" His eyes went wide. Kate sensed hesitation and underlying anger then it disappeared.

Adam nodded.

"Ok, I'll go ask. Thanks. You two have a fun night." He couldn't completely hide his disappointment but hurried over to Janice's table. She quickly agreed and they began dancing.

"That was very nice of you." Kate stood on her toes and planted a kiss on his cheek.

"Do I get a kiss every time I do something nice?"

"Maybe."

"I might have to rethink my bad-boy image then." He gave her his best tough look.

"Oh no! Not that." Laughing, they went to grab food and take a small break. Kate hadn't believed it was possible to have this much fun.

When they were ready to re-enter the dance floor, a slow song began. Adam wrapped his arms around her waist and pulled her close. She wound her arms around his neck, and they swayed to the beat of the song. He smelled like outdoors and fresh spice. The butterflies in her stomach ramped up causing her nerves to spiral out of control. She tried to squash the hope of what they could be together, but curiosity proved stronger.

She pulled back her head, and her eyes locked with his. A strange magnetic force seemed to bring them together. His head lowered to hers, and his grasp tightened. She held her breath, praying he didn't pull away. Her heart beat erratically as the anticipation overwhelmed her.

His lips brushed across hers. Then, they lingered. She tilted up her head to send the signal that she wanted this, too.

"Hey, you two." Alyssa interrupted. "This is still a school dance and lots of eyes will report what they see and create gossip. I noticed an awe-inspiring rotunda in the back gardens. Seems like a lovely spot to visit. Enjoy." She spun off again with her musical voice trailing behind her.

Adam smiled and dropped his forehead to hers. "She has a point, considering your papa is here and half the town. How about we check out that rotunda thing? What is a rotunda anyway?"

"Basically, a gazebo. I'm game." She'd been in this mansion many times in her life. One advantage was knowing all the exits. She took his hand and led him through the kitchen and out the back door. Luckily, the owners had turned on the exterior lights.

"Impressive." Adam held her arm to make sure she didn't trip on the stairs.

The rotunda had been built by Matthew Cavanaugh, the founder of the town, for his bride, Melissa. It'd been constructed out of stone. Despite the wear and tear of the years, a lot of the structure remained. Roses had been planted all around and flowed through its entirety. His wife had adored roses, so he designed this to be her retreat. He even renamed the town, Rosewood, for her love of the flower and her maiden name, Wood. Impressive couldn't adequately describe the majesty. The history and memories reached out to her. There were many secrets buried within these stone columns.

Stepping inside, the power of what had once been swept over her. "They had a good life here. An intense love that stood the test of time, just like this place." Kate leaned against him, and the old remnants of emotions infiltrated her. What would it be like to have an epic love story spanning centuries?

"I think you're right. Seems like the perfect place for a little honesty." Adam turned her so they were face to face, draped in the moonlight.

"What do you mean?"

"Kate, by now you know I have strong feelings for you, but we stay in this sort of limbo, afraid to move forward. I don't want that. I get that we're young and there's a lot of life in front of us, but we have something special. I can't predict the future and maybe this isn't meant to be forever. But what if it is? My feelings for you are strong. I'd like to believe we're in this together." His gaze deepened. "Your turn."

She sensed the fear of rejection and the courage it took to lay his heart out. Could she do the same? Was she brave enough? "Adam, I've been terrified to get close to anyone. They would like the image, but fear the *reality* of me. It's different with you. You see me for who I am and don't run away. Yes, we have the potential for something special. But with that, comes the possibility of great loss. That's my biggest fear for us. Pushing that aside, I'm ready for us to try being a real couple. I want to experience life, not hide from it. I have you and Alyssa to thank for that."

He pulled her in so tight she could barely breathe. "You won't regret it, Kate. I won't break your heart."

Not *intentionally*. She believed that much. Life had a funny way of changing directions, but she wouldn't dwell on things she couldn't control. She'd enjoy the chance of a relationship and take the leap of faith.

She leaned forward. Their lips met. After a brief moment of hesitation, he deepened the kiss. All sorts of feelings and thoughts ran rampant. Her chest tightened and a strange warmth flooded her body. The intimate connection surprised but delighted her. She didn't receive a backlash of his random thoughts or wayward feelings. Instead, she only felt his desire for her to like him. Crazy or not, she'd begun to fall in love before she could drive a car.

They stayed in the rose-covered gazebo bathed in the full moonlight for over an hour. As the night ended, he drove her home and gave her another goodnight kiss. She could get used to this new life she'd created.

CHAPTER 8

The screech of the front porch swing brought a smile to Kate's face. The sweet smell of blooming flowers surrounding the Ryan's home provided a strange sense of comfort. Spring weather had arrived, just in time for spring break. She enjoyed spending her first day off school relaxing with friends.

Closing her eyes, she leaned her head against the swing. This year had flown by, and she'd loved every minute of it. She, Adam, and Alyssa continued to meet daily in the library and assist others whenever the chance came about. They'd recently helped a classmate's mom raise money for medical treatments and caught a thief who turned out to be a homeless teenager. Linda had found him a foster family. Most of their cases had been small, but Kate liked it that way.

Her relationship with Adam also continued to grow. They probably seemed inseparable to outsiders. He held her close and spent time kissing her every single day. He never asked for more, eliminating any stress for anything more intimate. She had strong beliefs in that area and had no intention of rushing.

Over the last couple of months, she'd gained more control over her gifts, with Linda's help. However, the fights with her mother had also grown stronger. She feared Kate's closeness with Adam and Alyssa. Somehow, she could sense they were more than they appeared. Kate detected a little jealousy as well.

"Hey, kiddos." Linda stuck her head out the front door. "Dinner's about ready. Come set the table."

Adam laced his fingers through hers and gently pulled her up. He intentionally let her bump against him. Warmth spread through her. Sometimes, she feared he had cast a spell over her. How else had she become so entrenched in these uncharted waters? Luck had never been on her side. Maybe someone up above decided she'd suffered enough.

They all set out the plates and took their usual seats. Linda brought the meal to the table, and Luke said grace.

"Adam," Linda said, once the eating slowed down, "you've been a little restless lately. Anything you want to share?"

"Not really." He shrugged. "I don't know. I kind of thought that our opportunities to help others would grow bigger, but they've been a little boring. I guess I want more excitement with our cases."

Nodding, Linda turned to Kate. "What about you?"

"I'm content to handle the small stuff. When I think about all that could've gone wrong the first few times we helped people, it makes my stomach hurt. Don't get me wrong, I want to help whoever needs it. I'm willing to step outside my comfort zone, but I don't want anything to reflect badly on my family."

"I see reason in what both of you say. I've already had this conversation with Alyssa, whose response landed between the two of you. Fate brought the three of you together and gave you a purpose. Adam, you need to be patient. If you leave your heart and mind open to whoever needs help, you'll find plenty of action. Kate, you're still dealing with all the masks and wanting to stay hidden. To help others, sometimes you have to be willing to risk it all, yet believe it will work out for the best." Linda patted her hand.

"What about me, Mom?"

"Alyssa, my sweet daughter, you have the strongest spirit I've ever seen. You'll do a lot of good in this world and help heal those who have lost their way. I've watched all three of you closely this year, and you've all exceeded every expectation. I see an undeniable bond. It'll help each of you grow into wonderful young adults. A mother's greatest hope and comfort."

They quietly finished their meals. Kate felt Linda's love for her children and the amount astonished her. What surprised her more was the love Linda had toward her. She'd been a wonderful mentor and support.

Adam tapped his fork against the plate. "I appreciate all that. I do. The last few weeks I've felt something more is coming. I guess it has me on edge."

This time Luke and Linda straightened. Back to business. Linda sat still for a moment then met her eyes. "And you, Kate. What do you feel?"

She wanted to lie. Her dreams had gotten worse lately, and she couldn't shake the feeling of being watched. When she searched, she didn't find anything aimed in her direction. Linda had been so good to her, so she chose to tell the truth. "Something's coming. I don't know what, but we'll be challenged soon. The pressure inside me has been building for a while."

The second she finished speaking, the TV snapped on. Everyone gasped and froze.

"*In local news, a young girl has disappeared. Sources say she wandered into the woods near her home but didn't return. Search parties will begin searching for young Jessica at first light. Any volunteers are asked to check in at the tent…*" The news reporter gave a few more details, then it went to commercial.

Turning off the TV, Linda glanced around the table. "Anyone believe that could be a coincidence?"

Everyone shook their heads. Fear started to build in the pit of Kate's stomach. How had the TV done that? Why did she appear to be the only one at the table in shock? Everyone else acted like it had been completely normal to have a TV doing its own thing and didn't say a word about it. "May we be excused, Mom? I think we need to do a little research before I take Kate home." Adam started pushing away from the table before she could agree.

"Leave the dishes. Your brother and sister can take care of that tonight. If the three of you decide to get involved, promise me you'll be careful."

Alyssa kissed Linda's cheek. "Of course, we will." She grabbed Kate's hand and dragged her into the bedroom.

Here we go again.

They spent an hour finding all the details possible. The little girl was Jessica Cavanaugh, descendant of Mathew and Melissa Cavanaugh, founders of Rosewood. *No wonder all the media outlets were swarming.* According to witnesses and family, the child had a very adventurous spirit and would often wander into the woods, but she always came back home. Kate found it curious that she'd spent countless hours of her youth in the forest and suddenly became lost. Maybe she'd wandered too far this time. Something bothered her about the whole situation. The hairs on the back of her neck stiffened and goosebumps popped out across her arms. Not a good sign.

"I've been reading some of these articles about the family." Alyssa grabbed a notebook and started writing. "Apparently, there's been some bad blood between the family lines over the years. They fought over the Cavanaugh fortune until it was all whittled away on lawyers. The only remaining assets, like the mansion, belong to the town. The gazebo is the only part of the original estate that Matthew insisted had to stay with family. Technically, Jessica's parents are the current owners of the rotunda and surrounding gardens. Very strange."

Kate reached for the notes. "According to all the stories I grew up hearing, Matthew and Melissa spent countless hours there. Maybe they felt it should always stay in the family. It is a little weird that the family chose to live on a small farm on the other side of town. The forest area is massive and will take days for rescue crews to search it all. What should we do?"

"We volunteer." Adam sounded so matter of fact. She had doubts but let him explain. "Something led us to this case. I personally don't buy the "she wandered into the woods" theory. We have the skills to search and find her faster. If her life is in any danger, it's our responsibility to help. The police won't answer our questions or listen to our suspicions. As volunteers, we can do a little investigating ourselves. It won't hurt to help regardless."

"I agree." Alyssa turned and waited for Kate's response.

Like I have much choice. "I agree." Kate had a bad feeling this was going to be a lot more than they bargained for.

"It's settled. We'll pick you up in the morning." He pulled Kate to her feet. "For now, I better get you home before your mom starts getting worried."

The coming of spring hadn't prevented frigid morning temperatures. Kate's cheeks stung as her breath crystalized with every exhale. Adam walked over to sign them up and get all the appropriate items and instructions. She and Alyssa huddled together for warmth. It hadn't seemed as cold when they'd left the house, and their layers hadn't proved sufficient with the wind kicking up.

Teeth chattering, Kate tried to control her voice. "How does this work?"

"They assigned us to a group and gave us a map. We are supposed to slowly walk this quadrant looking for any signs of Jessica. In reality, we'll start with them and scan the area. If we don't sense anything, then we'll break off and find some of the more remote areas that the map doesn't cover well enough in my opinion." He would know considering his dad had been prepping him to be military since he could walk.

The first few hours were uneventful. Kate's feet started to hurt a little, but she couldn't pick up any mental energy from the girl. It didn't take a rocket scientist to figure out that Adam and Alyssa were hoping she'd find traces to lead them in the right direction. Their furtive glances gave them away. She'd be willing to bet that the girl hadn't been to this section of the woods in a long time. In her opinion, they were wasting their time. At least the sun had warmed things up a little, so she could feel her fingers and toes again. She shared her thoughts when they stopped for a lunch break.

"So what now?" Alyssa acted like she was stretching and led them to a tree away from prying ears.

"We're not doing her any good here." Adam searched the forest and referred back to the map. "I think we need to check out this area. It's further than she'd normally go and her parents insist she wouldn't go to that area, but, if she truly is lost, then it has to be an area where she's not familiar."

Kate made sure they weren't being overheard before they laid out their plan. "Ok, when we head back out, I'll distract them and we'll slip away. It still gets dark pretty early, so we need to watch our time." She didn't want to scare them, but she'd felt like someone had been watching them all day. Considering the circumstances, several people could be suspicious of her in this town, but she couldn't grasp any specific thoughts. However, occasionally a burst of anger broke through which led her to believe it might be outside this group. What did that mean for them if they split? She kept her mental radar on full alert. Even Linda wouldn't consider this playing it safe.

After slipping away, the first hour proved uneventful. Alyssa started complaining about her feet so they stopped for a bit. "How much further until we head back to the volunteer tent?"

"Stop whining, Alyssa." Adam ruffled her hair and she glared.

"I'm not whining. We've accomplished nothing except blisters on my feet. I checked the message boards. No one else has found her either. Maybe it's time we add a few more of our abilities into the mix. We're alone anyway."

By we, she meant Kate. She'd been scanning the whole time, but Alyssa believed she could do more. They needed to know if this was the correct location. Jessica only had a matter of days to survive. That took precedence over her inner doubts and fear.

She stepped forward and linked their hands to magnify her abilities. An unexpected malevolent energy swept over her. She gasped and broke the connection. "We're being followed. Whoever it is knows how to block their thoughts. I could probably break through but we're sitting ducks right now. We need to move toward base camp. Which way?"

Adam pointed and she closed her eyes. "That's where he or she is waiting. We'll have to find another way."

He studied the map and then motioned for them to follow. The new path led them deeper into the dark part of the woods. Her heart pounded. She tried to clear her mind and focus, but she didn't want to end up on the missing person list too. They moved as quickly and carefully as possible, but the negative energy stayed close. Alyssa held Adam's left hand and she held his right. That darkness moved closer. Obviously, it knew the area better than they did.

"It's getting closer, Adam."

"I know, Alyssa. What do you think?"

"We need to run. I sense a lot of rage and his mind is strong. I think it's male but the amount of crazy makes it hard to determine. Kate, what are you picking up?"

"Nothing good. I get the feeling he's pushing us in a direction of his choosing. Running may be our best bet but we won't be able to stay together. We'll slow each other down and be more visible." She wanted to go home. She wouldn't even mind her mother's yelling right now. Honestly, she deserved it.

"Look, the camp is straight ahead. He can't follow all three of us. Maybe if we cause enough confusion, it'll buy us time to rejoin the group. We're all connected mentally. If we get trapped, call out. The trees are thick on both sides. Use them for cover but don't lose sight of the trail." Adam pulled them in close. He kissed Kate softly.

Giving her one final quick embrace, he nodded. "On three. Let's do this quietly just in case. We need every edge we can get." He held out his fingers to his side. *One. Two. Three.*

They took off as fast as they could run. It didn't take long for Kate to realize the dark energy had decided to follow her. *Figures.* She stumbled over rocks and ducked under branches. Limbs pulled at her clothes and scratched her face. They also caught in her hair making her eyes water from the sting on her scalp.

She kept her mind open and focused. He wasn't far behind and wanted to capture her. Random thoughts kept popping into his mind, but her own fear made it hard to determine what was real versus imagined. She kept moving one foot in front of the other refusing to give up. Adam and Alyssa hadn't sent any distress signals, so it appeared she'd be having all the fun.

A dark figure burst through the trees and grabbed her. He placed a hand over her mouth. "Shhh. It's me, Kate." Adam had come for her. He must have sensed she'd been in trouble even if she hadn't reached out. "Alyssa's up ahead. Let's move."

The sun began to set and with the thick trees, they were losing light. Their pursuer didn't slow down. Adam pointed up ahead. "We're not far. I expect he'll show himself soon, if he intends to actually stop us."

Kate decided their best option was to outsmart the kidnapper. She'd spent her life preparing for attackers and this one probably knew where Jessica had been hidden or worse. Using their mental link to avoid being overheard, she sent them her idea. *"There's a clearing up ahead. We will split up in three direc-*

tions. I'll try to convince him to rejoin the others and see what's been discovered about Jessica."

"That's too dangerous, Kate." Adam held her hand tight as they continued hurriedly through the brush.

"But necessary. I'm the only one who can. He'll follow me."

"How do you know that?" Alyssa's voice entered her thoughts.

"I just do. Alyssa, you need to study everything you can about his aura and emotions. It might be our only hope to find the girl." Knowing this was the right thing to do didn't alleviate the nerves raging inside her.

She gave them the signal, and they split when they reached the clearing. Each found an area to hide in among the trees forcing the dark energy to reveal itself. It immediately focused on Kate and began searching for her. She felt it probing the area, desperate to find her.

Time to use one of her other abilities she hadn't shared with the others yet. Camouflage. She could blend her appearance to match anything around her or, at least, she projected that image so that's all a person could see. That included trees. She found one of the larger trees in the area and backed against it. Taking a deep breath, she exhaled and transitioned. Anyone walking nearby would only see or hear the forest. Hopefully.

The evil man crept closer. His negative energy sickened her. She'd only have a short amount of time to connect. If he discovered her messing with his mind, he might be able to form a permanent connection. She looked for a weakness or distraction to mask her presence, but his mental blocks were strong. Should she break through? What would it cost?"

Her own energy levels began dropping. Holding this type of illusion took a tremendous amount out of her. She had to act quickly or she'd be easy to spot. Panic started to rise. She struggled to control her breathing. *"Kate, the only clear fear I sense involves the missing girl."* Alyssa's message brought back a sense of calm.

Fear could cause a major distraction and that's what she needed. Focusing on the hooded man, she began pushing thoughts that information about the missing girl had been discovered. The police were discussing it back at the base. She even added in the sounds of walkie talkies to add to her story. At first, he resisted, but the fear of discovery weakened his mental blocks.

Kate didn't risk pushing into his thoughts and breaking the illusion. She couldn't maintain both. They needed him to leave, so they could survive another day. She pushed a little harder and felt the panic begin to rise. She decided to add a few uncertainties in his head. In his current panicked state, she hoped he'd interpret them as his own.

What if they find her? What if they find out about me? Do they already know? What have I done? I have to get out of here. I have to see what they know.

As his mind continued to weaken, she added more fear until his mind became frenzied. She urged him to go. To run. She saw a dark shadow moving to her left. He'd moved closer to her hiding spot than she'd realized. His indecision was evident. She held her breath when he looked straight at her beneath the large hood of his sweatshirt. She couldn't make out any features.

Please let my appearance hold for a few more minutes.

He took one step closer and then froze. She pushed the doubts and fears as hard as she could. If she reached out, she'd bump into him. He wanted to run yet felt compelled to stay near her. Total freak.

A walkie-talkie sound went off in the distance followed by walking sounds and dogs panting. She wanted to scream out but held her silence. The proximity of more people must have been the tipping point. He began to run deeper into the forest. She stayed put until every sign of him disappeared into the darkness.

She released the camouflage and nearly fell to the ground. Adam and Alyssa ran over. Adam swung her up into his arms and they began making their way back to the headquarters tent. Her words were jumbled from fatigue. "What about the people and dogs? I heard them. They should be here."

"Silly girl. You must be really tired." Adam kissed her cheek. "I made the walkie-talkie sounds and Alyssa got the dogs howling. We knew you didn't have much juice left in the tank. Your thoughts started getting a little scattered. Let's go home. Mom will have something to help and we can figure out what's going on. Lay back and rest. I've got you."

"Adam, I'm way too heavy."

"Nah. You're like carrying a feather." Strangely enough, she felt weightless. Too tired to care, she turned her face into his neck and fell asleep.

Kate woke up to the sounds of Linda clanging dishes and bustling around the house. Looking down at her phone, she realized that she'd been out for a good hour. At least her mom had been sent out of town on a business trip, so she was spending the night with Alyssa. Linda kept strict rules with Adam in the house, and Papa trusted her not to do anything inappropriate. She'd told him what they were working on.

"Drink this, honey." Linda brought her a mug with a steaming, weird looking golden liquid.

She took a sip and nearly spit it out. Alyssa laughed. "Tastes nasty but works. Drink up, girl. You need it."

Linda shook her head and then kissed each of them on the forehead. "I never said it tasted good. I'll leave the three of you to talk over today's events. Also, I expect you to be a little more careful in the future." She closed the doors of the study behind her.

"Wow. What a freaking day. Mom bought us a big board like we have at the library and said we could use this space as our own. Let's lay out what we know while our minds are still operational." Alyssa couldn't hide her excitement as she pulled out all the supplies and bounced around the room. Her endless energy and enthusiasm overwhelmed Kate at times.

She grabbed a marker while Alyssa danced around the room talking a mile a minute. When she finally took a breath, Kate interjected. "She's not in the forest, not alive anyway. I would've picked up something from her. While I distracted the creep, a random thought escaped about her not being nearby. That's what kept creating conflict in his head with the story I tried to create. He knew they couldn't have found her, but his fear of discovery made him shaky. My energy levels started to tank by the time his thoughts became more accessible. I'm thankful to both of you for giving him that last push to escape. I'm sorry I couldn't get more."

"No biggie. I'm not sure why he's focused on you. Maybe he could sense some of your mental energy or something else. Either way, that's something we need to remember." She tossed the marker repeatedly in the air.

"Maybe he's just crazy and searching for his next victim," Adam added.

"Ok, back to basics. We know she's not in that area. But we have no proof, so the police won't believe us. She's already been gone almost thirty-six hours. Time's running out. If they aren't searching beyond the woods, she'll die soon." Kate wrote all the facts down on the board. She began pacing and let the details run through her mind. It wasn't much to build a case on, but they had to find her.

"This town is pretty sizable. Where do we start?"

"I don't know, Adam. I guess with possible suspects and locations her family might be associated with. If we can find some type of motive, it could lead us to something more specific." She twirled the marker between her fingers.

"Speaking of this town, it's also very nosy. I think she'll be close to where she was kidnapped, and I think it had to be someone she didn't fear. If you make noise in this town, someone hears it. Yet, they can't find anyone who heard a thing. We also know her kidnapper is male."

"And he hasn't killed her," Alyssa interjected. "I got close enough to see that he doesn't carry the taint of death. Yet."

Kate pondered that a moment. "So, maybe this was an accident that triggered a desperation of sorts. That doesn't help with pinpointing the why. We may need to look for any motives revolving around the girl or her family, but also stay open to anything Jessica could have stumbled across during her usual adventures. Tomorrow, we'll head to the library and start answering some of these questions."

"What about the search?" Alyssa started packing away the supplies.

Adam shrugged. "What's the point? We know she's not there. We also know the evil prick isn't finished. He wants something else and doesn't want her discovered. It might be the perfect time to stake out some places based on our research. This isn't going to be easy and a lot is riding on our success. The police won't believe a bunch of kids, and we don't want to end up implicated in the whole mess. We have to be smart and document everything we find. Dad is helping me with that aspect."

Her whole life had been spent in this town. Kate couldn't imagine anyone capable of that much evil. It bothered her more than she cared to admit. If it ended up being a citizen of Rosewood, she'd never feel the same way about this place.

Adam pulled her to her feet. Alyssa slid out to give them a moment before the mom patrol came looking for them. "Are you sure you're alright, Kate? You scared me for a minute. I don't understand how he missed you, but I'm glad he did. I could swear he was standing right next to you on the other side of the tree. My heart nearly jumped out of my chest." He brushed her cheek and then pulled her against him. Guilt descended that she'd held back the truth of her abilities, but there were some things she wasn't ready to share.

She let his warmth wash away the drama of the day. His natural scent of spice and outdoors warmed her entire body. If she were honest with herself, a large part of her remained terrified of the crazy man with an intense interest just in her.

Adam helped her feel safe. *Cherished*. He captured her lips in a sweet kiss. She let the magic of the moment carry her away as he deepened the kiss.

CHAPTER 9

"Where do we even begin with all this crap?" Kate stared at the mounds of research sitting in front of them. They'd called ahead and the sweet elderly librarian had agreed to let them come in early. She'd had some work to do anyway. She'd also helped them gather tons of the town's history and old archived articles. It had taken Kate a minute to get the hang of the microfiche thing, but she finally figured it out.

She hadn't counted on quite this much information. It could take days to sort and prioritize if they didn't come up with a solid plan. Alyssa took charge of the overload and began sorting. She must have a photographic memory and the ability to 'speed read' because she could scan an entire document in seconds. Kate was fast, but not *that* fast. It humbled her a little.

Once Alyssa had most of it categorized, she started handing them some. "The quicker we get this finished, the sooner we find what's relevant. I've tried to pick up on any themes as I've glanced over them. My gut says we need to focus on the Cavanaugh family. There's a lot of motive built around money and the little girl is the next heir in line for parts of the estate."

The twins buzzed around each other but worked like a well-oiled machine. Though Kate felt a little left out, she tried to focus on what they were saying. Their years of experience trumped her years in hiding, and their minds fascinated her. They worked similar to a computer.

Probably a big advantage of having spy parents.

She couldn't prove they were spies, but they had to be something close with their lifestyle and secrecy. The more time she spent with them, the more she wondered what they were really about. Their parents had these mental walls she'd never seen before but wished she had them. Maybe one day she'd ask them to let her break through, not to take information, but to increase her skill.

Kate scanned the piles and saw a copy of Matthew Cavanaugh's last will. "Hey, this might give us some insight into the motive, or, at least, who benefits if something happens to the girl. And it might tell us if there are any other weird quirks he left behind." She sat down to read the lengthy document. The legal terminology gave her a headache.

After two hours, they'd managed to compile most of the information. Pretty impressive considering where they had started. A big clock kept ticking in Kate's head. The girl couldn't survive much longer without help. Maybe if she'd embraced her gifts years ago, none of this would be necessary.

"Stop blaming yourself, Kate. Your guilt is broadcasting for miles." Alyssa seemed pretty annoyed. "We've been doing this for a while and humans can be nasty creatures. They're unpredictable and sadistic. Most only look out for themselves. The worst characteristic is their intolerance for what they can't explain. It's why they fear you and made you believe that hiding was the solution. I'm sorry to be so blunt, but you've gotta move past this pity party and focus. A lot of evil exists in this world, and you've grown up pretty sheltered. It's not the same for Adam and me. Why do you think we've sacrificed our youth? Because we fight to protect those we can."

"Back off, Alyssa!" Adam snapped. "You should speak for yourself."

Kate had never witnessed this side of her before. Alyssa had a lot of hidden anger. It explained some of the frustration Kate sensed within her at times. They'd been dealing with this kind of stuff for years, and they'd been trying to give her space to catch up. With a girl's life on the line, she tried to understand the short temper.

"It's alright, Adam. I see her point." She turned to Alyssa and met her eyes. "But you need to see mine, too. We haven't had anything major happen in this town. Everyone takes care of each other, and, while they don't understand me, they have never been cruel or tried to harm me. So yes, it's hard for me to comprehend all the craziness you're talking about. I can see for myself that it took someone deranged to harm the child. But I don't go looking for trouble. I'm not from your world and there are times I don't want to be. And none of this arguing is helpful."

Reaching for some articles, Kate walked over to a window seat for some quiet. She wasn't sure why she'd let Alyssa rub her the wrong way, but this whole fiasco overwhelmed her. Maybe they were all antsy because the consequences of failure would be horrific. She scanned through as quick as her mind would compute, writing notes along the way. Another hour had passed by the time she finished her stack.

Alyssa quietly moved close and held out her hand to Kate. "I'm sorry. Really. We've lost someone before, and I guess it left a vicious mark on my soul. We were helping our parents find some trapped teenagers after they'd been playing in an abandoned house and it fell in. We couldn't get to the last girl in time. She died maybe ten minutes before we got to her. It's a nightmare that often revisits me. This whole thing is bringing back bad memories."

"I get it and I'm sorry you've suffered through that. But if a house collapsed, why all the anger toward us humans?" She wanted to understand, but Alyssa had held something back.

"Later we discovered that a jealous teenage girl had purposely caused the cave in. She'd actually studied how to do it and led them there. She'd been angry because they hadn't included her in their parties and they made fun of her at times. Still, like I said, people can be really stupid sometimes." Alyssa's eyes watered and she swiped across them to prevent an overflow.

"That's horrible. I've never known that kind of evil. So be a little patient with me. It's hard to grasp." Kate wanted to brush it off, but a new dynamic had been brought into the friendship. New doubts about their intentions toward her resurfaced, no matter how hard she tried to push them away.

"Of course, Kate. I'm so sorry. Are we good?" Her eyes seemed earnest, yet Kate sensed many more hidden emotions.

At Kate's hesitation, she grabbed her hands and silently pleaded for forgiveness.

"Yes, we're good. This whole thing has us all a little rattled." It gave Alyssa relief but Kate still had reservations. What if this is why they had befriended her? What if her mom had been right all along? If they were successful today, would they want bigger cases? In her mind, dangerous cases led to dangerous consequences. After this whole thing was over, she needed to sit down and really think about what she wanted to do with her future and how much she wanted to risk.

Adam rushed over. He'd given them some privacy but must've found something. It looked like he had a collection of blueprints in his hand. "I think I've narrowed down the possibilities of locations. Let's go over what we have. We need to rule out some, but it's a start. We've got to do this today." He started drawing circles on the town map.

Saving the girl came first. Kate pushed away all the doubt and focused on the task at hand. "If we can get close to the girl, I think I'll be able to pick her up. I'd say with her distress levels, she'll be broadcasting pretty loud. For me, I've figured out that the town will become the owner of all Cavanaugh property if the bloodline stops. That opens up a whole town full of suspects. The mayor announced a couple of years ago that the budget was tight. If someone did their research, then it could be a motive."

They laid everything out on the table, moving pieces around as new possible theories floated around. Alyssa picked up the details. "I studied the family tree. I don't think it's as simple as killing the girl to obtain the money. I found at least two cousins who could, technically, make a claim. On the other hand, it doesn't mean anyone else knows that. So, it doesn't remove any motive. Adam, have you narrowed down the buildings connected with Cavanaugh?"

"Maybe. There are three buildings left that were built by him. If we assume the motive is somehow tied to him, then these will be the most likely. The first is the library we're standing in now. The basement is rarely visited and would be the only possibility I could find on the blueprints. This place gets a lot of traffic, but it's possible. I say we check it out before we leave and cross it off the list."

"What's the second?" Kate wrote down all of the information for each building.

"The bank in the town square. It's been remodeled several times so not many hiding places exist except in the vault area. The vault is still the original but has been updated. According to the plans, there are a few hidden compartments that were closed off to increase security. It's plausible, but not probable."

"With the two you've already ruled out in your mind—prematurely I might add—you must be saving the best for last." Alyssa flung her arms in frustration. She tried to rein it in when Adam scolded her.

"Chill, sis. You're really starting to irk me." He took a deep breath and continued. "The mansion is the last area built by the founder. Most of the estate is the exact same. The problem is that it's massive and will take forever to cover all the hidden areas. When I studied the designs, there are dozens of secret areas. If we rule out the other two, the third is gonna take more time. We may even have to split up to cover more ground which is dangerous in itself." Adam laid out a map he'd copied of the Cavanaugh mansion and estate. He hadn't been kidding about the enormity of it.

Kate began to have doubts they'd find this poor girl in time. They packed up all the documents and returned what they could. Adam took pictures of all the schematics he'd found. At the very least, they had a starting point. With the motive and possible suspects still in the wind, she decided to pray for a miracle. They were going to need one. She refused to find the girl ten minutes too late, and she wasn't sure Alyssa would survive losing another innocent victim.

"Did you find everything you needed, honey?" Ms. Holt patted her hand and smiled. Despite her age, the lady's eyes always lit up like a child's when she talked about books and research. She'd helped Kate sort through a lot over the years.

"Yes, ma'am. Thank you for letting us come in early and for all the research."

"Glad to do it. It's such a comfort with all the young people starting to take an interest in the history of this town. It's important to know where you come from."

"It is." Kate hesitated. Something she'd said didn't sit right. "Ms. Holt, has anyone else been studying the same thing as us? We're thinking about a town project next year and would love to know of any like-minded students."

Ms. Holt looked through her records. "I wasn't here the other day, so my sister filled in. You know the one who lives part of the year down in Florida?" Kate nodded. "She mentioned a young man searching through similar documents. That's why I was able to pull most of them so quickly. They were still on my desk to return. I'm short staffed, so I'm not as spry as I used to be."

"Well, you do a fantastic job from where I stand. Do you happen to remember if your sister caught his name?"

"No, but I don't usually ask for it if they're just researching and not checking out. I wish I could be more help, dear."

Kate smiled and gave her a quick hug. "You've been wonderful. See you soon."

"Whatcha thinking, Kate?" Alyssa stopped her before they entered the basement door. "Those wheels are turning so fast, the steam will start pouring out any minute."

"I don't think this is a coincidence. Whoever was here wanted something from the Cavanaugh estate. The girl disappeared days after he looked at those documents. Ms. Holt and her sister are usually accurate with ages, so my guess is that we're looking for someone not much older than us. I feel even worse now." They crept down the steps slowly. The area wasn't huge, so it shouldn't take long for them to clear it.

Adam turned on his flashlight as they made their way toward the back. "Maybe this person discovered something more about the family fortune. After all the reading, there are still several family items not accounted for. What if this guy wanted to go on a treasure hunt and Jessica somehow got in the way?"

"Still doesn't make sense why Jessica would be there at all. She lives across town. What would she have seen over there that would have made the person bring her all the way back here? Kate opened her mind and searched for any trace of the girl. No one except them had been down there for months. Time to move on.

Adam led them back up the stairs, and they slid out the exit to avoid any questions. "Maybe Jessica stumbled across something at her home or saw him stealing something."

"That's a lot of guessing, and the *why* isn't important right now." Alyssa walked down the sidewalk. "Let's check out the bank and be done. I'm thinking all roads lead to the Cavanaugh mansion. The more time we leave for exploring it, the better chance we have of finding her."

A couple blocks down, they entered the bank. Alyssa waved for Adam and Kate to explore while she discussed a new bank account.

Once Alyssa had their attention, they crept toward the back section. Adam pointed up. "There are only two plausible places someone could be hidden and they are both located behind the vault." He moved them down a back staircase and opened a maintenance door. "One has a small opening from the top. I'll have to lower you in." He smothered a laugh at her expression.

"I'm probably already caught on camera doing something I shouldn't be. I don't want to be confused with a burglar." The last thing she needed was to become a suspected bank robber. Her mom would kick her out of the house for sure.

"I'll take care of the cameras. Dad taught me how to get around them. Don't worry. Hopefully, Alyssa keeps them distracted."

"Are you sure the cameras can't see us?"

"Yes, we learned at a young age how to not be seen." They crawled on top of a platform and he pointed at the opening.

Cringing, she held out her hands and let him lower her inside. So many things could go wrong with this plan and trust was not her strong suit. She quickly walked the area and determined no one had ever been in this section, at least not in the past couple of decades. She held up her hands.

When he hoisted her up, they fell slightly. Adam brushed some cobwebs out of her hair and held her close. His touch brought out the usual warmth throughout her body.

They stared at each other for a second then Adam cleared his throat and pointed at another section. "No distractions. I figure if I tell myself that enough, it'll sink in."

"Tell me how that goes for you." He'd definitely become a distraction for her.

They maneuvered through the tight space.

"Since you can't run away or avoid me," Adam whispered, "tell me what your plans are for the summer."

"Don't know. And that's the truth. I don't want to stay at home. Last summer nearly killed me. Master Instructor Austin has asked me to join his Taekwondo world tour exhibition. I almost went last year but don't want to be put on display. I'm afraid that's what it would become."

He slid around her and pulled her through a narrow entrance. Good thing she wasn't claustrophobic. "What about you? What are your plans?" Part of her didn't want to know the answer. A whole summer apart would probably mean saying goodbye to any relationship. She wouldn't ask him to wait when he'd probably meet much more interesting girls. She needed to mentally prepare.

He bent and kissed her nose. "You're so funny when pinned in a corner. You're not getting rid of me that easily. We have an agreement with our parents. They promised not to move until we graduate, but, in return, we agreed to pick productive camps each summer to hone our skills. Otherwise, we'd spend our senior year in training camps instead. There are a few that sound interesting, like forensics, computers, physical fitness, or other similar types. Alyssa and I will pick one for June and one for July. If you decide not to do the tour, maybe we could do the camps together."

"Maybe." She couldn't commit to anything because training camps didn't sound any better than the karate tour. If she did the camps, she would be with close friends, but did they need some separation? In a few short weeks, they'd be down to two years before graduation sent them in very different directions. Should she prepare by going her own way or take advantage of the time given to them? Great question, but she didn't have the answer.

"Let me know what you decide. I'll be waiting to hear," he whispered in her ear.

She felt her face flush in excitement. Luckily, it was dark so he couldn't see her reaction. They stepped into the back compartment and searched quickly.

Kate stretched her mind to evaluate all the energy residue that had been near the vault. Each individual had their own form of energy signature similar to a fingerprint. She'd studied Jessica's when they'd been near her home. Kate sorted through all of them but each belonged to a bank employee. She'd known most of them her entire life, since her mother did her banking here.

Sighing, she shook her head and they silently made their way back to the main floor. "I guess there's only one place left, if our theory is correct."

"Are you surprised?"

"Not really. A part of me knew it would end there. Since the ball, I've known something would lead me back to the mansion. I just hoped it wouldn't happen. We've made pretty good time. If we hurry, we can search a large amount of the property." Kate grabbed Alyssa who'd been entertaining the entire branch with a delightful story. Her dazzling personality had made her the perfect distraction.

"Since we're rushing to the car, I assume the mansion it is."

"Yep." Adam opened their door and ushered them in.

When they arrived, most of the caretakers had gone home for the day. They usually only worked in the mornings and then locked everything up. The only exception occurred when visitors would ask to schedule a tour or to host an event. It'd become an excellent source of income for the town.

Kate remembered where the gardener stashed his key, so they went in through the back entrance. "It's not likely she's anywhere in the house. There's too much…" A strange sensation caught her attention. They weren't alone. Somewhere on this property, the kidnapper also searched for something. After being so close in the woods, she wouldn't mistake him.

"Kate? Where'd you go?" Alyssa snapped her fingers in front of Kate's face.

"The guy from the forest is here. He doesn't seem to be aware of us yet. I don't sense anger or fear. I think he's looking for something. On the positive side, I'd say we're close to finding Jessica. On the bad side, there's no way he's gonna let us just waltz outta here with her. He'll fight to keep her hidden and we'll have to fight to save her. We don't have enough proof to call the cops. Once we know her exact location, we can fabricate a story and say we heard screaming or something like that." She scanned to see if he was nearby but couldn't get a solid location. He faded in and out like a bad radio connection.

"What freaking luck." Adam shut off his light to avoid detection. Even though it was the middle of the day, the heavy curtains darkened the manor.

"Let's move through the house quickly." Alyssa's voice held a sharp note of urgency. "With all the staff, it's not likely she's here. Adam, did you see anything to help in those house plans?"

"Most are already on the tour. There's a hidden staircase off the master and a hidden pantry off the kitchen. These are the only two I haven't heard mentioned on any of the tours and they're not listed on the pamphlets. Let's head up quietly. We'll check the master first."

Kate kept a hand on Adam's back as they progressed toward the bedroom. Once Adam unlocked the door, he immediately pulled up the plans on his phone and headed to a wooden bookcase. He gently pushed it to the side. They walked down the hidden stairs. It led them down to the kitchen. She hadn't picked up any human trace. Although they had a much bigger mouse problem than they realized. She never intended to be that close to the ghastly little creatures ever again.

"Well, we made it to the kitchen." Alyssa kept wiping off her arms and legs. The spider webs had totally freaked her out. Adam distracted her while Kate grabbed a large web from her hair. Alyssa shivered and locked her jaw in place to cover the discomfort and fear.

Adam opened the pantry, and they walked to the far corner. They moved stuff around, trying to find the entrance. Kate finally pulled on a light fixture and the wall slid open. The space reminded her of a small coat closet. Jessica certainly wasn't being held captive in this tiny space. Maybe they were overthinking and giving this creep too much credit.

"What if this guy stumbled upon something? Ms. Holt had to dig for the blueprints. No one has studied them lately. It's not going to be some secret room in the house. With all the workers and tourists, there's no way he stumbled into a hidden room. He'd have to figure someone could hear her screams. He wouldn't take that risk, right?" Kate tried to put herself in the kidnapper's shoes. Where would you hide a little girl and never be discovered?

"If we go by that theory, then the same holds true for the barn." Rubbing his hands across his face, Adam leaned against the counter. His sister wasn't the only one suffering from memories of the past. "We can stick our heads in to rule it out, but we know the outcome."

"Depends on his knowledge of the place." Shrugging, Alyssa held open the back door, and they raced to the barn. Kate stepped inside and searched for any signs, but came up empty. Adam and Alyssa met her in the center with similar results.

Alyssa paced the floor. "Where to now? Did anything else pop up on the plans?"

Desperation rose high in Kate's chest. She'd believed, once they were here, she'd be able to connect with the girl. What if it was too late? Another hour had passed, and they were out of ideas.

"Back to basics." Kate shook the doubt away and motioned for Alyssa to hand her a pencil and paper from her backpack. "Our kidnapper didn't do as much research as we did. Alyssa, you mentioned earlier about treasures. What if this is just about money? With Jessica being a descendant of Cavanaugh, it's likely her parents possess pieces of the family fortune like heirlooms handed down. Maybe he saw a piece worth a lot of money or put the puzzle together like a treasure hunt."

"Wait a minute." Alyssa spun the paper around and pulled out some of the notes they'd brought. "When we looked at the archives, there were several mentions about family fortune and Matthew's vast collection of artworks. Actually, several old documents referred to priceless pieces."

"So what?" Adam came up behind them to watch as Kate took over and hurriedly mapped out everything they were saying.

She pointed. "In all the later articles, the items aren't mentioned. They weren't listed in the estate or will. The question is, where are they? Did Cavanaugh become so worried about the works of art being stolen that he hid them away? If so, where?" Kate let all the information race through her mind, trying to connect the dots. Where should they be searching? A massive room of priceless artifacts wouldn't be easy to hide.

It struck her. "My God. It's the gazebo. I felt something hidden there the night of the ball. But it doesn't make sense, where would you hide stuff in the gazebo?"

"You have to look below the surface. I've got it!" Alyssa grabbed a sheet of her notes. "The builder for Cavanaugh was Reginald McMurray. I looked him up when I saw all the work he'd done specifically for this estate. His specialty was hidden tunnels and rooms. One of his most notable works happens to be an underground hideaway the size of a small warehouse. And get this. He always used iron in his work. His favorite saying about his art pieces or buildings was *To find the true beauty one must look below the surface*."

Kate jerked up her head and met Adam's eyes. "In the books your mother gave me, they all said iron and similar strong metals could interfere or interrupt psychic energy. I bet that's why I can't pick her up. I'm not skilled enough to punch through it. We'd have to be incredibly close."

"Kate, you seem to have the closest connection to this insane pervert. Can you track him? Can we get to the gazebo?"

She closed her eyes. He hadn't left the grounds, but tracking him proved difficult. "He's here. I think he's near the wooded area. I can't get a clear reading though." If they wanted answers, they had no choice but to go to the gazebo.

Adam motioned them to follow. They crept up slowly. He moved in first to secure the area, then told them to join him. "I don't see anything special about this place. I don't want to waste time on the wrong location. Kate, can you sense anything at all?"

Blocking out the fear and sound of her own pounding heart, Kate opened her mind and searched for any trace of the girl. At first, she only found silence. Then, a whimper echoed in her mind.

She latched onto the trace of energy. Jessica had lost consciousness. She'd become severely dehydrated and probably had a touch of hyperthermia. Kate forced a better connection to assess for further injuries. The girl didn't appear to have any broken bones, but her breathing became more and more shallow with each passing minute. They had to find a way to rescue her, or she'd die.

She transferred the details to Adam and Alyssa. "I don't know if she even has another hour left. It's bad down there. Her mind isn't focused. I picked up that someone forced her inside and she fell, but that's it. We need to find the entrance!"

Kate tried to keep the panic out of her voice. After connecting to the girl, she couldn't lose her.

They searched under every rock and in every crevice. Tears flowed down her face as desperation grew. She crawled from one side of the floor to the other. She stopped in the center and hung her head. Wiping her eyes, she stared at the ground below. The patterns intrigued her. One seemed out of place from the others.

What if…? Could it be that simple?

She motioned Adam over. Alyssa followed. "What is it, Kate?"

"These patterns don't quite align. What if we turn this one to match the others?" Kate reached down and slowly rotated the designs made of iron.

A loud click echoed, causing her to jump. The ground shook and a trap door unlocked. The second it opened, Kate fully connected to Jessica. "She's definitely inside here."

The darkness stretched in front of them. They should probably call for help, but the girl couldn't wait that long. Her body already showed signs of shock. They stared at one another hoping a better idea would strike, but, it didn't. Alyssa texted her parents all the information, knowing they'd handle calling for help.

"On three?" Adam held out his hands. She and Alyssa each grabbed one. Luckily, the opening was big enough for them to enter together. They nodded and the breath caught in her throat.

"One. Two. Three." They jumped into the black abyss.

CHAPTER 10

Landing with a thud, Kate winced as the pain radiated up her spine. When they hadn't seen any stairs and the shadows didn't seem too far down, jumping had been the only option. She moved her flashlight across the ground and noticed drag marks. A ladder had once stood at the entrance. "It would appear our creep knew how to navigate this place."

Adam stacked a couple of crates and jammed a rod into the opening. "We don't want to end up stuck here. Where is she?"

"Further back. Listen." Soft cries indicated she'd regained consciousness. They needed to be careful not to spook her or cause additional distress.

"Holy crap! Look at all this stuff. It has to be worth millions of dollars." Alyssa took a few pictures to document the items. Paintings, vases, and jewelry lined the walls. Kate could only imagine what all they'd see with full light.

They remained silent as they inched their way farther down the tunnel. Kate tried to keep track of how deep they'd gone, but it proved difficult in all the darkness. Finally, Jessica's crumpled little body came into sight.

Adam rushed to her and draped his hoodie around her. Kate wrapped hers around her legs. She didn't have any obvious broken bones or open wounds, but she hadn't eaten for days.

"I knew you'd come for me," her small voice stammered. "I heard you searching." Her eyes locked on Kate.

She bent close. "Jessica," she whispered, "I'm Kate. We're here to help you. Everything's going to be okay. We just need you to hang on a little longer. Can you tell me what happened?"

Jessica shook her head, too weak to talk anymore.

Alyssa opened her backpack and pulled out snacks and water bottles. "Get her to drink a little water. Then, we can try some food. She needs enough to make it to the hospital, so they can provide exactly what she needs to recover. Kate, see if she'll let you check her over before we move her."

Patting her arm and kissing her forehead, Kate quickly assessed Jess' body. She didn't sense any pain from movement, except a few bruises from when she'd been pushed inside. It would take a lot of time for Jessica to be able to speak of her days down here and the horrors she'd endured. Kate figured she'd simply access her thoughts to obtain the whole story. No need to make her relive it.

"Her parents owned an ornate heirloom box. It's been passed down for centuries. Her cousin paid a visit and noticed the markings were a map for the flooring of the gazebo. He went back to the house to steal it, and Jess walked in on him. Her parents were out back, so he snuck her out the front door and threw her in the trunk of his car. He brought her here to cover his tracks. Once he figured out how to open the trap door, he tied her up and pushed her inside. He's been gathering some of the pieces. Probably plans to head out of town to pawn them and cash in on his new fortune."

Alyssa smoothed the girl's hair. "Who would do such a thing while this poor girl withered away? That's a whole new brand of evil," she muttered.

"We'll get you home, honey. Hang in there." Alyssa whispered into Jessica's ear. Then, she turned to Kate and asked "Who did this?"

The words barely formed in Kate's mind to answer. Shock had infiltrated her system. "Jimmy."

"Say what? You mean the timid kid always drooling over you who can't take a hint?" At Kate's nod, she gasped. "Just to be clear, the one who can barely tie his own shoelaces and turns red anytime you get within ten feet?"

Once again Kate nodded and shrugged. She had no words.

"You've got to be kidding me!" Adam's anger rapidly escalated. "I should've pounded that kid at the ball when he asked you to dance. I knew something was slightly off about him, but he backed off. Could we have prevented this?"

"No, this isn't on any of us. I can't see anything else or exactly what sparked this move toward insanity. The cops can ask when they find him, which will hopefully be after we get Jessica to the hospital. I've been so focused on Jessica that I lost my connection with him, so we better get moving." Kate leaned over. "Jess, Adam is going to lift you. It might cause some pain, but you'll be free soon."

She whimpered but sluggishly wrapped her arms around his neck.

He held her carefully, and they began walking back to the entrance. When they were a few steps away, a large bang signaled someone had kicked in the rod.

"Jimmy found us," Kate mumbled, not wanting to further upset Jess. But now they were all locked inside.

Alyssa had texted her parents their location, but would they figure everything out? Too bad there was no cell connection in the pit to send them an update for urgency. With water and food, they'd possibly bought Jessica a little more time, but she needed medical attention.

Kate refused to let this girl die in their arms. She walked underneath the trap door and sensed the faint echo of his energy. He hadn't left. Why would he stick around after accomplishing his task?

"Jimmy! You let us out of here right now! Do you hear me?" She tried to add a mental push to make sure he got the message. Dealing with iron proved more difficult than she realized. If she made it out, she had a lot of training to do.

A crackling sound caught her attention. An intercom had been added into the wall. "My darling, Kate. I've done all this for you. I've created the perfect world for us. No one will ever make fun of you again or spread rumors about you. We can be together forever."

What the hell was this crazy idiot talking about? This had nothing to do with the Cavanaugh fortune! He'd done all this because of his obsession with *her*? She may not have a clear idea of her future but, it sure wasn't him! Guilt crept in as Jess's breathing grew more shallow.

It's all my fault...

"Snap out of it." Alyssa shook her and grabbed her chin, forcing their eyes to meet. "This isn't on you. None of us sensed the depth of his obsession. Our best bet is for you to keep him talking and give my parents time."

Adam kissed her cheek. "You can do this."

She walked to the intercom and pushed the button. "Jimmy, I don't understand what you're doing. What have you done that would bring us together? You know I hate violence." She hoped he'd feel a sense of guilt and open the door.

"That wasn't part of the plan, my love." His voice sounded like he'd entered dreamland and never walked back out. She fought the nausea rising and held back the biting remarks he deserved.

Keep him talking. "What plan?"

"For us. I've been watching you for years. The other kids were so cruel, but I knew we were destined to be together. I studied all the books I could find on telepathy and mental energy. I learned to build strong walls to protect you."

That explained why she hadn't been able to fully connect or see the dangerous obsession. Maybe she just hadn't wanted to. "Protect me from what? So far, the only danger I'm in is being locked inside here."

"All the people in this town. They've never appreciated you and all you could offer, but I do. I did my research and discovered the Cavanaugh fortune by accident. I had no clue how to access it until I visited my cousin's house. I truly had no intentions of harming little Jessica. When she caught me stealing the box, I didn't have a choice. I had to make sure she didn't tell anyone about our escape plans. Why do you sound angry?"

Where to begin. Now they were escaping together? He'd built an elaborate delusion. Adam rotated his hand for her to keep him talking. She didn't want to hear more. She wanted out of this whole nightmare.

"Jimmy, I don't need an escape."

"Yes, you do. Everyone knows you're gone after graduation. One of those weird government facilities will probably take you away and use you up. The world is evil and you'd never fit in. I'm using the money for us. I'm reconfiguring this whole hidden area. It's massive just like a house. I've already added an intercom and plan to add piping so we have plumbing. Once we move in permanently, it'll be just like living in a castle. I'll provide everything you need. I wanted to surprise you after graduation, but things got a little out of hand." His voice sounded earnest and held regret.

In his mind, he'd built an entire fictional world around her and his belief that he could provide her a better life. Focusing on the positive, at least, they'd foiled his plans to kidnap her after graduation. On the downside, he still had the upper hand and could kill them all.

How do you negotiate with straight up insanity?

Kate racked her brain for a solution, but came up empty. Adam had placed Jessica back on the ground. Alyssa held her, trying to keep her as warm as possible. Despite their efforts, she continued to fade. They had to get her out of here.

"Jimmy, you need to let me go." Kate tried to sound stern, but even *she* could hear the fear in her voice.

"I'm sorry, but I can't. You've aligned yourself with the enemy and you must be punished."

"I don't understand. What enemy?"

"Adam and Alyssa!" His hate for them radiated in his voice. "You were just fine hiding from the world, until they came along and forced you to be something different. They've infected you and I'm not sure you can be saved."

Kate moved away from the intercom. Her hands shook, and her knees were weak. Adam pulled her against him for support. She'd read about obsession but nothing this severe. His whole concept of the world was an elaborate illusion he'd been building for years. Her relationship with Adam had sparked this whole mess.

"He's mentioned a lot about preparing for your future together. See if you can keep him talking about the plans." Alyssa held Jessica close and brushed her cheek. More and more color faded from the child's face and her eyes became glossy.

She found a new resolve within herself and went back to the intercom. "Jimmy, what can I do to make this right? You've worked hard for so many years to bring us together. But I didn't know. Are you going to just give up on us?"

At first, he didn't answer and she feared he'd left. He sounded torn when he spoke again. "I've loved you my entire life. I got my black belt in karate to protect you and to be worthy of your skill. I bought a new car and I've been studying engineering to turn this place into a home. It's why I needed the money. I planned a great life for us. I guess I never told you any of that though."

He paused. "I'll give you one chance to save our love. You have ten minutes to decide. I'm setting my timer. If you'll agree to leave everyone else in the vault, you can exit. We'll seal them in and share this secret until our deaths. It's more powerful than a marriage ceremony. I know you want to save everyone, but this one time you have to choose. Choose me and live. The clock's ticking."

"I guess I have to make the deal and try to outsmart him on the surface." Anxiety had paralyzed her chest, making each breath a chore.

"Absolutely not." Adam started pacing. "We need him to open the door and lure him inside."

Alyssa motioned them to be quiet. "Lower your voices. We don't want to be overheard or cause Jessica any additional stress. None of us doubt that he's crazy, but he's also smart. Look at what he'd constructed so far."

"There's no way to lure him in," Kate whispered. "He'll be expecting that. I wish I knew if your parents were on the way. The only chance we have is for me to get outside this hole and gain control or, at the very least, buy us time for help to arrive. Seriously, do either of you have any better ideas? I'm listening." Her heartbeat continued to increase as the reality of what she had to do sank in.

A loud bang startled them all. Adam had tripped over something while trying to find another exit. It wasn't going to be that simple. The minutes continued to disappear. Her nerves weren't improving. If she didn't trick Jimmy, they'd all die down here. The choice became clear. Even if she had to sacrifice herself, she'd save three innocent people.

The intercom crackled, signaling time had run out on her decision. Adam's face displayed a mixture of anger, fear, and desperation. He yanked her against him, then passionately kissed her. It felt like saying goodbye.

She cleared her throat, straightened her shoulders, and punched the button. "Jimmy, I've made my choice. I choose you. After hearing all the sacrifices you've made for me, how could I make any other decision? I've said my goodbyes and expressed my sorrow. I'm ready." She forced the words out, hating every single syllable.

"Come to the door. I'll drop down a rope and help you out. If anyone tries to escape, I'll lock everyone inside forever." The door rattled as he aligned the symbols.

The rope fell to the ground and she grasped it to begin climbing. Jimmy pulled her up. She didn't look back at Adam or Alyssa for fear she'd chicken out. Before she reached the top, Alyssa reached out and connected to her mind. *"Hurry Kate. I'm not sure what's wrong with Jessica but it's getting really bad. She won't last much longer. Be careful."*

Kate sent her reassurance. She squinted as the afternoon light of the sunset hit her eyes. "Hello, Jimmy."

"I've waited for this moment for years. You'll finally be mine forever. We'll have kids and spend every minute together." His eyes didn't quite focus on hers. He'd become fully trapped in a make-believe world. That could be a great advantage for her.

Taking a deep breath, she fought the vomit rising. He'd just described her worst nightmare. He'd never have that kind of access to her body. What now? He wouldn't be releasing them out of kindness. Honesty was all she had left.

"Jimmy, if you've watched me for years as you say, then you know I can't let others die while I live. It's against my nature. Why did you suddenly decide this was all necessary?" She tried to inch closer to the trap door. If she could open it, Adam would find a way out.

"It's your fault the timeline changed, Kate. I was content to wait until after graduation when you would be ready. Then you let them into your life and changed. I had to act. To save you. Anyone could see you were falling for him."

"Who are you talking about?" She desperately tried to keep him talking.

"Adam. He rode into town and swept you off your feet. He had a car, money, and movie star looks. All the girls were drooling but he honed in on you. You never noticed me after he waltzed in. Even at the ball, you couldn't spare one dance for me. So, I did my research and moved up the plan."

What he needed was a straitjacket. She'd happily put him in one. Help better arrive soon or she'd be in big trouble. "I've never been one to chase money. Why did you think that would change me?"

He began pacing. His agitation had increased the more she questioned and breached his fantasy world. "Don't you see? I did everything for us. I've watched your every move, learned to fight, learned about all the mental crap you do. The last piece was financial stability and we have that now. Take my hand. We'll leave and never look back. You and me." Jimmy extended his arm.

Kate couldn't maintain the charade any longer. She didn't know if anyone was coming. What if Alyssa's mom hadn't gotten the message? She steadied her nerves and prepared to fight. "Jimmy, that's not the life I choose. You've described a prison, and I need freedom. You'd destroy me. Is that what you really want?" She gave one last shot at reason.

"Don't confuse me with your lies." His tone changed to anger and desperation. "You tricked me. It's all his fault. He changed your heart and stole you from me."

"I was never yours to steal. Sorry, but I need you to open the door. *Now.* I've had enough of your whining and delusions to last me a lifetime." Kate added a little compulsion and bent down to open the latch.

Jimmy kicked her in the side, knocking her back a few feet. A different person stared back at her. His eyes had dilated so they appeared nearly black, and his face had become twisted with rage. If she ever met the devil, she imagined he'd look like this. Her compulsion had failed. He'd been more mentally prepared than she'd expected, or maybe insanity took a different type of control.

Luckily, with all her training, she'd been able to take the hit and get back on her feet quickly. They danced around each other. He advanced with a punch. Kate blocked and responded with a front kick. He deflected her advances. She took a steadying breath. Her fear had made her less focused. He wasn't on her level, and she could easily kick the crap out of this asshole.

A strange calm washed over her as she launched forward. She threw several kicks in a row followed by an uppercut. He blocked most, but she'd landed a few. He appeared rattled, so she went in full force. She spun low, sweeping his legs. She tried to pin him but he rolled out of the way. Before he could get fully upright, she took a running start and knocked him down with a flying side kick.

He got up slowly. She ran in to finish him, when he flung something toward her head. She jerked to the side and followed its path into a column of the gazebo.

Throwing knives?

He'd brought weapons and she had none.

Great. This is ludicrous.

Aiming another in her direction, she barely ducked out of the way in time. She wouldn't get anywhere playing hide and seek. Gathering her courage, she stood and faced him. He launched a third knife straight at her head. She snagged it out of the air and sent it spiraling back toward him. It jammed into his shoulder.

He wailed in pain, but it didn't slow him down. His mind didn't register the discomfort long. He let loose two more knives. His desperation had made him sloppy. Kate easily caught one and the other didn't get near her. He tried to dive at her, but she jumped onto the ledge of the gazebo and flipped over him. She aimed a kick toward his chin, causing him to fall backward.

With blood dripping down his face, he snarled. "You think you can defeat me? I've been preparing to overpower you for years. I knew it wouldn't be easy and you've proved worthy. But that won't be enough to save them. The designer was a clever man but with a simple wrench in the works, the vault will be locked forever. No one will suspect anything. You can't save them, Kate. You never could."

Kate caught his meaning. There must be some sort of kill switch or locking mechanism in the design. She dove to cover the intricate design at the same time he launched another knife. If he damaged the rotation, they'd be trapped. She extended her arms as far as she could.

She screamed as the knife cut through the side of her hand.

Tears sprang into her eyes as blood dripped down her hand. She'd blocked the opening for now. They were safe. He hadn't pulled another knife so she hoped he'd run out. Ripping off a piece of her shirt, she tied it tight around her hand to stop the bleeding.

The inner rage she'd struggled to contain her entire life came bubbling to the surface. She launched into another attack. This time she showed no mercy. She landed every punch, kick, and sweep until he landed in a bloody heap at her feet. Her training and instructor's teachings returned a sense of calm before she did something she couldn't take back.

Jimmy crawled to the bench seat and tried to pull himself up. "You can't win, Kate. I can't allow it."

"Looks like I'm doing a hell of a job so far, Wacko."

"I feared you might be able to overpower me, so I decided to bring a backup plan."

Oh no. What did that mean?

He turned and aimed a gun at her head.

Holy crap!

Time to use the gifts she'd been born with because she hadn't learned how to dodge bullets. She studied the energy surrounding him to assess his mental state. She also focused her ability to move objects and brought the process to the forefront of her mind. Ignoring the gun pointed at her face, she pinpointed all the elements around them to help her escape. Her mental compartments had proven useful for more than creating masks and hiding.

He pulled the trigger. She slowed the process down with her mind, so it appeared to be moving slowly in her eyes. She deflected the bullet. She didn't have a lot of practice with anything this advanced, but she held her ground. She tried to center her energy on the gun but couldn't remove it from his grasp. She didn't have quite enough control.

However, she could control the mind. He had strong blocks but she understood mental capacity and could manipulate it. "Jimmy, drop the weapon and surrender." She sent a strong wave of compulsion.

He laughed at first, yet displayed signs of hesitation. Building up his mental walls, he tried to break free from her enthrallment.

Not today. His mind wasn't any different from the countless others she'd manipulated and studied in her lifetime. She visualized the energy waves moving between them. His aura weakened and she ramped up the compulsion.

Tossing back her head and narrowing her eyes, she stood straight in front of the gun now aimed at her heart. "You will drop the weapon. Drop it *now.*" She kept repeating the words adding more and more compulsion until she felt his mind literally split from the pressure.

He lowered the weapon against his will. She disarmed him and threw the gun far away, wanting no part of it.

He whimpered. "How did you do that?"

"My will is stronger than yours." She discovered some twine in his bag and tied him up until help arrived.

Having returned to the gazebo floor design, she turned the piece until it clicked into place. Then she threw down the climbing rope. "Adam, send Jessica. I've taken care of Jimmy. He can't hurt us anymore."

The rope wasn't necessary. Adam had already built a makeshift ladder with which to escape as soon as the door opened. Passing Jessica up to her first, he then helped Alyssa out. All of them being back on the surface allowed Kate to process the damage to her own body.

Considering what she'd faced, she hadn't suffered anything that wouldn't heal with time. A few bruised ribs, a sore ankle, and a gash in her hand were minor in comparison to death or an eternity with that freak show.

Sirens in the distance signaled the whole nightmare had come to an end. Ambulances, fire trucks, and police cars surrounded them. They'd had just enough time to concoct a plausible story. In their interviews, they each stated that they'd come to check out the gazebo to hang out and explore the area and heard something underground. They found the latch and heard the girl below. Believing she must've fallen inside, they went in to bring her out.

Kate told the police that she'd convinced Jimmy to let her out and that's when she learned what all he'd done. She also told them about the weapons and that she'd disarmed him. Many of the police officers took classes at her studio and knew her capabilities, so they didn't really question her story. Jimmy's constant howling and professions of eternal love mixed with rantings of craziness provided all the confirmation the cops needed.

When she watched him hauled away in the back of the police car, relief poured through her. Her mind finally allowed her to believe it was over. They'd saved Jessica and themselves. A terrifying success that few in this town could've accomplished.

The EMT treated her on site because she refused to go to the hospital. She wanted to go home and didn't even mind if her mom yelled at her for a while. The comfort and safety of family beckoned her.

Adam dropped her off at her house. "Are you sure you're okay?"

"I guess. Physically, anyway. It'll take a while to get all of Jimmy's crazy delusions out of my head." Kate could barely keep her eyes open. She tried not to fall asleep. "I'm tired and sore, but counting my blessings that I'm alive. Was it your parents who sent the cavalry? I saw them pull up among all the other vehicles."

He pulled into her driveway and shut off the car. "Yeah. After Alyssa's cryptic text—remind me to give her a lesson on proper texting to parents by the way—they went to the police. Alyssa only sent that we sensed Jessica and were going under the gazebo to check it out. They didn't know we were in serious trouble or they would've come themselves. It took a while to convince the police that we'd managed to find the girl in a completely different location. Mom thinks they believed it to be a prank at first. My parents were insistent and threatened to come by themselves. Then they heard the gunshots, since they're located in the town square, and everyone came running. When the gun fired, it nearly gave me a heart attack. I never want to feel that helpless again, and I don't want to lose you, Kate."

He placed his hand behind her neck and slowly pulled her toward him. He kissed her while emotions of fear, exhaustion, and love poured off him. "It's alright, Adam. We're all okay, and we saved the day."

"We almost didn't. It's my fault. I pushed us to seek bigger things. I never imagined it would all fall onto you to save us." He rested his forehead against hers.

She gently tugged on his ear. "Don't go giving yourself that much credit." She brushed his cheek with her uninjured hand. "You didn't turn on the TV that night. A higher power or guardian angel led us to her. There's no other explanation. We were the only ones with the right tools to save her. Sometimes we're challenged to complete the impossible. Your mom taught me that. We saved a life, maybe more, because Jimmy can't hurt anyone else. Stepping outside our comfort zone made an impact just like your mother told us it would. I don't blame you for any of this. I care about you, if you haven't figured that out yet."

"I started to suspect a little glimmer of feeling. I care about you, too." She laid her head on his shoulder and he held her for several minutes before she exited the car. She sensed he wanted to say more about his feelings but cut himself off. Maybe when things calmed down, they'd both be ready to confront their emotions.

The trauma of the day had begun to take a toll on her body. Her hand burned and ached all at once. She knew her mom would have her sitting in the doctor's office first thing in the morning. That was the main reason she'd refused the hospital tonight. She'd be there soon enough.

"Cadence." Her mother half sobbed her name.

Both her parents embraced her tight. Her dad hadn't touched her in years out of fear of her abilities. She must've really scared them tonight.

They guided her into the kitchen. When her mom saw her bandaged hand, she started sobbing again.

Kate wasn't sure what to do, so she let them hold her and fret over her. "I'm sorry, Mom. I tried to be careful. But I had to help the little girl. You know it's not in my nature to turn my back on someone needing my help. She was so weak."

Her mom patted Kate's back. "Shh. Don't apologize. Linda called just as I arrived home and filled me in. I can't believe your luck. Imagine finding the missing girl while exploring the old Cavanaugh mansion. You've been there a million times. I guess you're prone to those coincidences. You're very fortunate

Adam and Alyssa were there to help. I can't comprehend little Jimmy being such a nutcase. It's why I've always said it's important to hide what you're capable of."

Kate wanted to point out that Jimmy had figured it out, but decided to leave it be for now. Her mom ran around the house helping with everything possible. But Kate drew the line at the bathroom.

In her bedroom, her mom had laid out pajamas and turned down the covers. As Kate changed clothes, she noticed a new dolphin figurine on her desk. She'd collected them her whole life and her mother brought her one each time she traveled to a new city.

When she stopped to think, she had to admit there had been a lot of good times in her childhood before her mother's fear bombarded their relationship. And maybe a little of her own irrational anger impacted it, too. Maybe they could eventually find their way back to happier times. The thought lifted her spirits.

She climbed into bed and exhaustion overtook her. She managed to turn out the light and drifted to sleep.

CHAPTER 11

Kate woke up to a horrible throbbing pain in her injured ankle. At some point, she must've cried out because her mom sat at the end of her bed and had begun to massage the area. It brought back memories of when she'd been young and had those crazy dreams every night. Her mother would sit beside her and rub her back while singing softly. She'd provided immense comfort during a very confusing time in her life.

In a moment of weakness, Kate allowed herself to feel her mother's emotions. Tears sprang into her eyes as the overwhelming amount of love overflowed. She shouldn't have doubted her mom's feelings. She'd let years of frustration and anger prevent her from seeing the real reason behind all the fighting.

If she were being honest, a big part had been her fault, too. When her parents had pulled away not knowing how to deal, she'd pulled away harder to avoid the pain of their distance. "Thanks for being here. Mom, you know I love you, right?"

"I pray I keep your love every day even when I know I don't deserve it. Kate, you scared me tonight and made me face some harsh truths and to evaluate my behavior. That kid could have destroyed my world in a matter of seconds. Once I knew you were safe and on your way home, it forced me to see how far I've pushed you away the last couple of years. I've tried to mold you into my vision for your future, but only alienated you in the process. I ignored who you're meant to be and it's only caused us both pain. I won't be perfect, but I promise to try and make things better between us." Her mother hugged her for the first time in years without flinching in fear.

Kate wasn't naïve enough to believe her mom finally accepted all her gifts, so she prodded a little to get the whole picture of where things stood. "What is it you see for me? I'd genuinely like to know. Tell me the truth."

She watched a quick flicker of irritation cross her mother's face, but when Kate winced as she sat up, her mom's expression turned soft. "You always need the explanation. You were never satisfied unless you had the whole story. I've always admired your tenacity. The complete opposite of myself. The call to protect others and find justice runs deep inside you. I've been foolish to ignore that piece of you. Instead, I should've helped you find a way to use it and turn it into a good career. With Adam and Alyssa's influence, I see you joining the police force or military. Maybe eventually becoming a lawyer. You'll learn discipline and satiate your desire to help others. That's my two cents anyway."

No mention of her abilities. Had they been inadvertently omitted or purposely evaded? Her mother had found a way to reconcile her skills with normalcy. The longer Kate thought about it, the more she admitted her mom might have a point. Even if she mastered all of her gifts, where did that leave her future? Where would she go or fit in?

"Mom, Adam and Alyssa have been talking about some summer camps like forensics and other law enforcement stuff. Would you be okay with me going with them? It'd give me a chance to see if that kind of career would be a good fit. You're right that I don't have a clear direction yet. I think I've been afraid to look. This opportunity could change all that."

Leaning over, her mom kissed the top of her head. "I'll talk it over with Dad, but I don't see why not. I'll admit I didn't care for your new friends at first. I let my suspicious mind overlook how they've changed you for the better. You're no longer hiding at home or in the library. I see happiness instead of pure anger at the world. They've allowed you a glimpse of what a normal life could mean for you."

She walked to the door then turned. "I know I don't say this as much as I should, but I love you, Kate. And I'm so proud of you."

If she only knew Adam and Alyssa's family like Kate did, this conversation would've gone very differently. Instead, it'd paved the way to spend more time at the Ryan home and learn from their experiences and knowledge. Who knows? She could end up going with one of them after graduation. Papa always told her there were no coincidences. He believed everything provided a step toward a predestined path. Was this hers?

She took the aspirin her mom had laid on the nightstand and drifted into a semi-painful deep sleep.

"Are you sure you won't join us this summer, Kate? It's an excellent way to travel and see the world." She'd been helping pack up the studio all afternoon. Master Instructor Austin always secured everything for the summer break.

She nodded. "I'm sure. It's a great opportunity, but not for me. At least, not yet. I also wanted to talk with you about training next year. I won't be able to come here as much. I get my license in a couple of days, and Mom says I'll need to have a job to cover insurance. I've got a couple of camps coming up. I'll return at the end of the summer. I should be able to find the time for at least a few hours a week."

Master Instructor Austin stayed silent and seemed a little lost in thought. She hoped he wasn't really upset with her. A smile lit up his face. "I have the perfect solution. Our enrollment has grown drastically the past year and I need a new instructor. You earned your collar last year. How about you work for me and help train the next generation? It's the best of both worlds."

"Are you serious? You'd hire me for a real job?" She tried to control the excitement building inside her. She couldn't ask for a better opportunity.

"Absolutely. It's perfect for both of us and you get paid to do what you love. Is that a yes?" He grabbed some paperwork for her to fill out over the summer.

"I'd love to. Thank you." She placed the papers in her bag and went back to cleaning.

"By the way, you never told me how Jessica is doing or what happened to all the artifacts you found."

Kate had visited her yesterday and brought her some ice cream. "She's doing great. Luckily, she doesn't remember much from her time down there. I watched a little TV with her and she read me her favorite book. I think she's going to join one of our karate classes to help rebuild her confidence. Her resiliency is inspiring. I don't know if I'd be that strong after what she endured.

"As for all the artwork, her parents and the city decided to display all of it in a brand-new museum dedicated to the Cavanaugh family. They're building it on the estate. Jessica will have quite a nest egg if she ever needs it." She wiped the perspiration off her face as she stacked the mats. Everything had worked out, including Jimmy being sentenced to a psych ward indefinitely. The town hadn't wasted any time completing his trial.

"Kate, before you head out, I wanted to tell you how proud I am of you. You've come full circle from the angry preteen who walked through my doors with a massive chip on her shoulders. Have a great summer. I'll see you in August. I'm looking forward to it." He laughed and pointed toward the window. "I think your ride is here."

Adam danced around the car like he was in a scene from a musical. Then, he flipped up his pretend collar and leaned back against the car. His smile caused her stomach to do a somersault. He didn't try to look gorgeous, he'd just been blessed by nature. His styled hair, tall muscular build, and magnetic personality created a deep attraction within her and with most other females. But he only had eyes for her. Spending the entire summer with him was the largest perk to all the camps they'd chosen.

Kate ran and jumped into his arms. He scooped her up and spun her in the air. "You'll never believe what job I'm going to have when we get back home this summer!"

"You already found a job? That was fast!"

"Yep. Master Instructor Austin offered me an instructor position starting in August. I get to work with the Little Dragons group mostly. It's perfect. Everything has worked out." She leaned her head back against the seat and let memories of the past year play through her mind.

A few minutes later they arrived at the Ryan home. She'd maintained the routine of at least one Ryan family dinner a week. She'd also made a concerted effort to spend more time with her own family. She and her mom still bickered a ton, but a new understanding had blossomed from the near tragedy at the Cavanaugh mansion.

Of course, the town had cashed in and added all the details to the tour. People were driving from miles away to hear the story of hidden treasure, kidnapping, and a daring rescue. The mayor had put his own special spin about the police arriving just in time to save her from death. Her memories worked a little differently, but she didn't begrudge them the glory. The whole ordeal had brought revenue into the town. At least, their rescue had provided an additional silver lining.

Tonight had been pre-determined to serve as her *birthday party/everyone's going off to camp* party. All of Adam's relatives had come to celebrate and to meet her.

Alyssa ran to the car and a tall beautiful redhead followed her. Adam exited the car and swung the girl around. She laughed and returned his embrace. Then, she grabbed Kate and wrapped her in a big bear hug. Kate recognized her as one of their cousins from the photographs inside the house. This family didn't hide from their emotions and they'd somehow managed to corner the market on good looks. As she glanced around the yard, she could have easily stumbled into some sort of modeling academy. It didn't help her self-confidence any.

Kate motioned for him to visit with his cousins after he introduced them. So many emotions and names had overwhelmed her. She snuck in the front door and headed to the study for some privacy and to recharge. She'd become more comfortable in her own skin, but couldn't completely let go of the masks that had become her coping mechanism. Adam and Alyssa had breached her inner mental sanctum, but she wasn't ready to expand on that for now. Deep down, she simply wanted them all to like her. She didn't trust her real persona to deliver those results yet.

Walking quietly to avoid any more introductions, Kate slid up to the door, hoping to go unnoticed. She heard voices inside. She tried to back up quickly, then froze. A tingle ran up her spine. She couldn't shake the feeling this conversation might be about her.

"Our mission is to protect and this little adventure nearly got her killed. She needs to learn, but surviving is the main goal." Kate recognized the lady speaking as Adam's Aunt Jill from the family photographs, his mother's mysterious sister and business partner.

"You think I don't know this. Maybe this whole issue is what we were protecting her from. It could be over."

"Please. Wishful thinking is not helpful. Look at the facts. From where I'm standing you put her in excessive danger. Your reaction time was pathetic."

They stared at each other for a few seconds. Kate made herself invisible. Eavesdropping usually wasn't her style, but she needed to hear whatever they were saying.

An angry spark lit up Linda's eyes. "The facts are, my dear sister, that she's fine and stronger for the experience. A person with her gifts isn't going to move through this world unchallenged. How else would she be prepared when things really get difficult?" She ran her fingers through her hair, clearly exasperated. Kate had only seen the calm collected side of Linda. This side scared her.

Jill grabbed her shoulder. "I've shared what her future holds. While it didn't provide much detail for us to go on, we both agree her destiny is something stronger than anything we've witnessed. What I'm suggesting is that you use a little more caution or teach her to be better prepared. Can you at least handle that? We can't afford to screw up."

Linda bristled and gnashed her teeth. Kate wanted to smack the woman. Her bossy nature rubbed her the wrong way, but some of the words must have resonated with Linda because she began to calm down. "Maybe you have a small point. I can't go around proclaiming what we are and what we do. We don't live in your sheltered world. This town doesn't invite the unusual. Luke and I decided not to tell the kids our full mission, but it worked out. They've created an unimaginable bond, they're happy. When's the last time you've seen them this content to be who they are?"

Jill shrugged without responding.

"I didn't know if Alyssa would ever recover when we lost that girl. She became overwhelmed by the senseless violence and it left her very bitter. Kate is healing her. They're healing each other. There are many different ways to save and protect a person. I love you and don't mean to be rude, but I've got this and don't need or want your interference. My family has never failed a mission and that's not changing. However, it's going to take more of our time than I realized. Are you good to handle the other cases and track the rogue group that keeps causing trouble?"

Hands on hips, Jill looked like she was planning a nasty retort. Then her face softened and she shook her head. "I can handle it. The girls are almost finished with their training and they'll join me in the search. Peter's handled most of the tracking so far, but has other projects that need attention. The world's a crazy place, and this girl's an important piece. Don't let your love for her become a distraction. That's all I'm saying. If you need help, call me. We can be here in minutes." The last comment surprised Kate. She thought they lived farther away.

Jill paused and her intense expression made Kate shiver. "Linda, she's special. She'll make a difference in this world, maybe even save it. I fear what will happen if we lose her physically or mentally. She contains so much strength but will endure equal parts pain. That continual dream she hints at could be the key or could be completely unrelated. See if you can find out more."

"Adam and Alyssa will watch over her. They don't need the details because they love her. I trust them. I also know she'll tell me her nightly vision when she's ready and not a second before. She's suffered a lot. My goal is healing, then we can sort out the future."

"And what if it all collides? Or if they aren't meant to be in her future long term? How much more pain will that cause them all?" Jill's eyes began to water like she could see destruction on the horizon.

"If that happens, they will each be better for the time they had and adventures shared. You never did really grasp the complexity of human nature or its resiliency. We've got this."

"I hope so." Jill led Linda from the study. They walked in the direction of the kitchen.

Kate plopped down in the chair. Not much doubt she'd been the focus of that conversation. They'd known about her before they even moved here. What had it all meant? How could one person save the world? It didn't make sense and why was interpreting her dream so critical? Dreams didn't predict the future. She'd had minor visions in the past and her nightly occurrence was different. She didn't plan to share it anytime soon and have it dissected. It might get worse and she didn't want to risk it.

One of Papa's sayings popped into her mind. *For peace to exist, you start with showing kindness to one person.* Maybe it worked the same for saving lives. She'd prevented Jessica's death. What if she, in turn, saved others in her lifetime? Domino effect. No way she could be sure if that's what Jill and Linda meant, but something to think about. What if one act of bravery or kindness could impact the whole world?

Her mind spun with new possibilities. Papa believed every event in life served a purpose. Adam and Alyssa had appeared at a point in her life when she'd almost buried herself behind the walls of illusion. They taught her balance and the importance of helping others. Obviously, they hadn't been informed of the grand plan either. That brought her comfort. She'd made new friends and discovered a new direction in her life. She'd found a purpose for the gifts bestowed on her at birth. What if fate had given her a guardian angel to help her find her way out of the darkness just as she had helped Jessica?

Instead of hating my abilities, maybe it's time to embrace them.

"Girl, what are you doing in here all alone? It's hard to have a guest of honor without the guest part." Alyssa danced around and motioned for her to follow. "We're here to party, birthday girl! Get your butt in gear and move out here to celebrate!" She paused and cocked her head to the side. "You okay?"

Kate nodded and smiled. "Just contemplating life."

"Find time for that later, like, when you're sleeping. Let's go have some fun and cake. Gotta have cake!" Alyssa pulled her out of the chair.

"Yes, bossy. I know your love for sweets." Kate followed her, but kept all the other thoughts locked away. She didn't want to dampen Alyssa's mood.

"I know. I love being in charge. Adam always tries to be in control, so I have a slight tendency to be overly assertive or, at least, that's what Mom says when she's lecturing me about it." Alyssa's whole demeanor had brightened since the rescue. She'd hidden behind her bubbly personality in the beginning just as Kate had hidden behind the masks.

The more time Kate spent around her new friend, the more she could see the serious side of her nature. Alyssa wanted to help others and was ready to jump into the fight with both feet. She'd been trained her whole life to rise above and be the adult. That's exactly what she'd become. They'd missed out on some of their childhood just like she had. That's why she related to them so well. While most teens focused on their favorite outfit, the best parties, or what was trending next, they'd been given responsibilities to keep those teens safe. A heavy burden, but a worthy one.

She didn't consider them heroes or vigilantes which was mentioned in the local papers. Instead, they'd become protectors of the innocent just like the name they'd given themselves before they understood the potential of its meaning. A sense of rightness washed over her like she'd unlocked a piece of herself. For now, she'd consider it a sign that she'd chosen the correct path.

Linda had spared no expense. The cake had three massive tiers, and balloons filled the room. They sang an off-key *Happy Birthday* and celebrated until late into the night. Kate had never been around this much family partying. They talked and joked. The boys wrestled around.

A plan started to formulate in her mind. She'd ask Papa for a family end-of-summer get together. She'd invite Adam and his family. Maybe the whole lot of them. Should make for an interesting occasion. At the very least, she'd be quite entertained. She tried to suppress a laugh at her mother's possible reactions.

"You look like you're planning some serious mischief, Blondie." Adam wrapped his arms around her waist. "Care to let me in on it?"

"Nothing big. I'm thinking about getting our families together for a barbeque. I'll tell you more about my grand plan later." He couldn't hide the surprise in his eyes. She'd been so determined over the past year to keep their families apart that she didn't blame him for being confused.

"Really? So not like you." He led her out under the stars and pulled her back against his chest. He rested his chin on her shoulder.

She turned and kissed his cheek enjoying his warmth. "It's time, I think. I plan to keep you for at least a little while longer."

"A little while? Not good enough. My plan is to keep you close for a very long time." He turned her in his arms to face him. "Truth is, I love you, Kate. I know we're young and there's a lot of life in front of us. But you've stolen my heart." He drew her closer.

Kate's heart nearly beat out of her chest. They were young, but stranger things had happened. They'd proven they'd stand by each other no matter what. She could do this and embrace the honesty within herself. "I love you too, Adam. I fought it every step of the way, but you persevered. I honestly don't know how it happened, but I'm sure glad we ended up here."

He connected them in a deep sweet kiss that curled her toes. She'd never given much credence to romance, but she'd been wrong. Warmth spread throughout her body and she craved the growing bond between them. His hands glided up her back and pulled her close to the point not a millimeter of space remained. She completely relaxed in his embrace, reveling in the miraculous events of her life.

"How does it feel to be sixteen and legally able to drive?" Papa led them toward the garage.

"It's great. Between us, though, I think I'm more excited about the camps this summer, but driving is huge and a little scary. Borrowing mom's car is a whole new level of terror." Why on earth were they heading out here instead of his workshop? She didn't like all the darkness and cobwebs.

He pointed to a large canvas to the side that she'd never noticed before. "I thought that might cause a few issues, so I wanted to give you this before you head to the forensics camp."

It couldn't be. Her adrenaline pumped as she ran over and flung off the canvas. He'd rebuilt an older Toyota Camry. She loved the blue exterior, and it had gray interior. "How?"

"Adam helped me rebuild the engine. I made him promise to keep it a secret. Finding time when he wasn't around you proved the biggest challenge. And Kate, your dad helped, too. Maybe it's time to mend that fence as well." She stayed silent. They'd never had much of a relationship but maybe he did care more than she realized. She'd focus on her mom first. She could only handle one mountain at a time.

He pulled the cover back over. "We don't have time for a test drive today. I don't want you to be late for the bus."

Wiping her eyes, she tried to hold back the tears. He'd always done so much for her. She couldn't imagine how her life would've turned out without her grandparent's unending support and love. "Thank you so much. I love you."

"Love you too, Katie girl. Let's get going. I've already put your bags in my car and Grandmother packed a bag of goodies for you. As soon as you get back, we'll take it out for a spin."

"You've got it. After all, you taught me to drive. I can't wait!" He laughed as she squirmed in the seat all the way to the drop-off. She couldn't help it. She had her very own car and a job to cover the insurance.

For once she didn't fear the emptiness of summer or returning to school. She'd found balance and happiness. Fate had given her an amazing turn of events and so much more to come on the horizon.

Kate ran to Adam and thanked him profusely. She'd already sent a text to her dad. "I can't believe you kept it a secret."

"Alyssa deserves credit, too. She had to keep you occupied so I could slip away. You deserved the surprise and your papa deserved to be the one to bestow it." He grabbed her bags and carried them to the bus while Kate turned around and embraced Alyssa, thanking her, too.

Her mind processed the last several days. The conversation between Linda and Jill still bothered her, but she hadn't shared it with Adam or Alyssa. Their parents seemed to share everything with their children, yet lately she'd gotten the feeling they didn't share as much as she'd believed. Why all the secrecy? Why did Jill know so much about her when she'd only met her once? Why did she need special protection? Maybe it all related to her nightly dreams. She wanted answers and feared them at the same time. She made a mental resolution to enjoy the summer and search for the truth when she returned.

A strong wind caught her attention and goosebumps broke out across her arms. A time for change.

She stepped back and took a long look at the town she loved and hated. A feeling that something would drastically change caught her off guard. Whatever the challenges to come, she knew they'd face them together.

Clearing her head, she walked over to her friend and boyfriend. Her new life. "Here's to the best summer ever!" She held up her water bottle.

Adam and Alyssa raised theirs to meet hers in the middle. "Ditto."

And it would be. She felt it all the way to her bones. They loaded up and headed toward new adventures.

Continue Kate, Adam, and
Alyssa's journey in *Force of Nature*

About the Author

J. L. Lawrence lives near Nashville, Tennessee with her family including three rambunctious children. She loves reading and exploring new places. Her imagination has always provided her greatest adventures. Her oldest daughter begged for a story that they could build together. She wanted relatable teenage angst with plenty of magic and mystery. This led J. L. to create a new YA series, *Path to Destiny*. Please explore the website and check out her Facebook and Instagram.

authorjllawrence.com

Made in the USA
Columbia, SC
03 July 2019